Running Home

Running Home

A Heart's Haven Story

Katie O'Connor

Snarky Heart Press

 Created with Vellum

DEDICATION

Since no good deed goes unpunished, I dedicate Running Home to my adorable and somewhat bossy sisters, Jean and Andrea. I hope you consider it a compliment that our constant bickering provides both fuel for my fictional arguments and affirmation that family love can overcome anything.

Special thanks to the talented ladies in my writing group. You've given me a ton of fabulous ideas and slammed the brakes on some lack-luster ones. You're a source of inspiration and motivation. My critique partners, Shelley Kassian and Brenda Sinclair, are the best (even when they refuse to put up with my shenanigans.) You girls rock!

Natalie Walker cast a quick glance in the rearview mirror of the cherry red 1957 Corvette convertible she'd taken from her lying, abusive husband. The mirror revealed nothing. There wasn't a headlight behind her for as far as she could see. Not that she could see very far.

She breathed a sigh of relief. No one was tailing her.

Clusters of towering pines crowded the edges of the narrow highway, frequently meeting overhead to block out the last of the daylight. Heavy clouds hung low over the mountains, almost low enough to be fog, and threatened rain at any minute. The twisting, turning mountain road hid nearly everything except the immediate terrain. Daylight faded further, and the almost nonexistent moon cast no light. It was dark and getting darker fast. She should have stopped earlier instead of choosing to drive on.

She wasn't going fast. She wasn't even doing the speed limit, but it felt as if she were flying, as though the speed could help her outrun the demons chasing her. No, not demons. Demon. Singular. Her husband. Could she escape him this time? Could she save herself and her son from a life of decadence and abuse? She never should have agreed to marry him; every single day, she regretted bowing to her father's dictates and accepting Stanley's proposal.

The small car bottomed out on another rut in the ancient blacktop. Her head bobbled alarmingly, and her neck wrenched painfully. Blacktop, ha. Once upon a time, it might have been pavement. Now, it was more like a series of washboard ruts and potholes with intermittent flat spots.

She spared a quick glance at the car seat beside her. Three-year-old Mathew slept soundly, undisturbed by the rough road. His short blond hair was tousled and moist where his head rested against the car seat. It was a gift that her son was such a good child and traveled so well.

She hit another rut, and the bottom of the car bounced alarmingly. Didn't they do maintenance out here in the back of beyond?

"It can't be much farther." Desperate longing for the relative safety of her friend Belinda's ranch was the only thing that kept her going.

With a flash of lightning, the heavens opened. Her car's headlights barely penetrated the raging downpour.

"Dammit." What looked like yet another patch of loose gravel appeared ahead. She gave her sleeping son an apologetic look. "I wanted secluded, but this is ridiculous." She braked in preparation for the gravel. The car bounced painfully as she crossed the rough spot.

There had been a dozen cars to choose from. Her husband, Stanley, had a passion for expensive cars, and this one was no exception. Almost all of his vehicles had every bell and whistle, including GPS and onboard computers. If there was a gadget, his cars had it. Except for this one, a classic Corvette, which was completely stock; perfectly maintained exactly as it had been the day his father had purchased it. But really, would it kill him to have a GPS in the glove box? Sometimes, her husband was an idiot. Her soon-to-be ex-husband. As soon as she figured out a way to ditch him without endangering her son, Stanley was history. She was through with him.

The road smoothed out, so she stepped on the accelerator and eased the car back up to a decent, but cautious speed. There wasn't a hope in hell she'd find the ranch at this time of night, but she wanted to hit a town and find a hotel before total darkness descended on the mountains. Not that it could get much darker. How far could it possibly be to the exit she was looking for? Okay, maybe, she should have bought that map back in Golden, instead of scratching down some directions. She was conserving her cash. She had to stretch it as far as possible. If she used her credit cards, Stanley would be able to track her. The car's lack of an onboard computer system was why she'd chosen it. He couldn't track her. Ironically, it meant she lacked the GPS she so greatly desired.

She fingered the bruise darkening her eye; the swelling and tenderness made her wince. She never wanted to see him again. She'd reached her limit. She refused to be his punching bag any longer, even if it meant she and Mathew had to spend the rest of their lives on the run. Nobody would hurt her son. Ever.

The previous evening had been the final straw. Stanley had taken his anger and frustrations out on her. Again. Thinking of the abuse made bile rise in her throat. She swallowed the nausea down and shivered despite the heat blasting from the car heater. She was cold, sick and scared.

She tried to keep her mind on the road, but it kept flitting back to the night before. She hunched deeper into herself, shoulders wrapped defensively forward.

Drunk, yet again, Stanley had smacked her around. But her luck had turned after he'd punched her. Stanley had passed out on the marble floor of the kitchen, and she'd thrown a few things into a bag, scooped Mathew from his bed and bolted. Initially, she'd run on adrenaline and then a short nap in a roadside turnout as she fled Vancouver, crossed British Columbia and headed into the mountains toward Alberta and the safety of her friend's ranch.

A shiver of unease and fear skittered down her spine when she thought of him catching up with her. She forced herself not to hyperventilate, to breathe calmly and slowly. If he ever found them, he'd make her pay for her disobedience. Her arm still hurt where he'd wrenched it last week and most of her body ached from bruises. He had a knack for hitting her in places where the marks wouldn't show; a skill he'd mastered after an acquaintance had noticed the first bruises she had acquired at his hand.

All the times he'd threatened her, had forced her to bend to his ways, Natalie had suffered in silence. Scared and alone, she'd ignored his increasingly frequent bouts of physical abuse. She could tolerate a lot, but the first time he threatened their son, she'd started plotting their escape. She'd tried once, but he'd caught her when she'd stopped at the bank for cash. That was when he'd changed the alarm code on the house, effectively making her and their son his prisoners, prompting her to seriously stress-manage and strategize her this moment and her escape. Like his cars, the alarm system was nothing but the best, and Natalie swore it was designed as much to keep her in as to keep the riffraff out.

Constant surveillance made it hard to conceive a plan of escape. He'd never let her out of the house without the bodyguards he claimed were there for her protection, but she knew better. It wasn't because he was rich and had earned almost celebrity status in Vancouver; his behavior was all about controlling her.

He wanted her to be as submissive as his father had been to his mother and sisters. The only time she was unsupervised was when she left Mathew at home. That memory made her claustrophobic. Stanley knew her too well. She'd never leave her son behind. Keeping Mathew at home had been the only chain he needed to effectively imprison her.

But he hadn't counted on her need to escape, to be free and live her own life. She'd gathered the funds, a few dollars here and there. Then, all she had to do was be patient until he made a mistake. The nest egg was small. She couldn't survive on it for long, but the money would be enough to take her away from him and let her live until she found a job and childcare for Mathew. She had to be frugal.

Fortune had smiled on her two weeks ago when her wheelchair-bound mother-in-law had spilled her tranquilizers. Natalie had slipped half a dozen in her pocket while helping pick them up. She'd lived in fear Stanley would find the pills in one of his random searches of her room. He'd never discovered them or the cash she had wrapped in plastic and taped to the inside-bottom of a box of tampons.

Tense and twitching with the fear of being discovered, she'd waited and waited, trying to hide her impatience and fear until he slipped up.

Last night, Stanley had been high on himself, gloating over pulling a fast one on one of his many enemies. He had started hitting the bottle hard and fast in celebration, toasting himself again and again. She hadn't joined in at first, until he punched her in the eye for not participating in his gloating.

When she'd finished recoiling from the blow, she'd realized it might be her best chance for escape. Natalie had encouraged him, taking tiny sips of her drink, pretending to get drunk. Thankfully, he had agreed to her suggestion to take a walk in the yard and had forgotten to reset the alarm when they came inside. Finally, she was able to slip the tranquilizers into his drink, and before long, he was out cold on the kitchen floor.

He went down hard, banging his head against the marble tile. She'd worried she had killed him. Killing him might have freed her from the abuse, but being convicted of murder would separate her from Mathew.

Relief had flooded her when Stanley's chest rose and fell with the slow inhalations of breathing. She'd stared at him without moving for several minutes before it sank in this was her chance and she'd better not blow it.

She tossed a few essentials into bags for her and Mathew,

grabbed the keys to the only car without an onboard computer and bolted.

Now, here she was seventeen hours and hundreds of kilometers later, on a crappy country road in the dark in the pouring rain. She'd driven continuously, stopping only for a quick nap and to feed Mathew. She hadn't seen another car for over an hour and was beginning to suspect she'd made a wrong turn somewhere. She was headed into the back and beyond, but somehow, she hadn't expected the road to continue climbing like this.

She had no option but to continue driving and hope she ran into another town to confirm her directions. Damn, why hadn't she bought that map? Her cell phone had a built-in GPS, but she'd left the phone at home. There was no way she could use it. Lord knows, Stanley's goons and PI would be tracking it. All she wanted now was to be out of the rain and to find Belinda's place.

Natalie cast a silent thank you to the heavens that her husband had never met Belinda. Natalie doubted he knew her childhood friend existed, but she was grateful for the twist of fate that had kept them from meeting. At least now, she had someplace to run where he wouldn't find her.

Now, if only she could find Belinda's ranch. She'd never been there. In fact, except for a few emails, she hadn't had much contact with her friend in the years since finishing college. Sneaking around behind her husband with a secret email account and secure private browsing that didn't track the sites she visited hadn't sat well with her innate honesty. It was, however, the only way she had been able to maintain contact with Belinda.

Thinking about the pictures Belinda had sent, Natalie knew she was off course. The ranch had been flat and a great part of it treeless. It certainly wasn't anywhere near here, in the heavily forested mountains.

She'd definitely made a wrong turn.

Through the driving rain, Natalie glimpsed another stretch of loose gravel ahead. Easing off the accelerator, she slowed the

Corvette. The car fishtailed alarmingly when she hit the first bit of gravel. Cautiously, she slowed further and finally regained control. At this rate, she'd never get to a town. Cresting the next hill, she was blinded by an approaching vehicle's high beams.

"Shit." She gripped the steering wheel tighter.

Her headlights must have surprised the driver of the pickup hurtling toward her in the wrong lane. He veered toward his lane and then back toward hers. Instinctively, Natalie edged toward the ditch on her side of the road as the pickup roared past.

Her back tires struck the soft shoulder and the car slid toward the ditch.

"Shit, shit, shit." She punched the gas, hoping it would spin her clear. She threw her arm out to brace Mathew in his seat. She hated he was in the front, but the minuscule Corvette was a two-seater.

The tires caught, and she careened back onto the road surface and slid toward the other side. Her heart pounded, she clutched the wheel in a death grip and she slammed on the brakes, hoping to avoid skidding off the other side of the road. The Corvette fishtailed again and exploded off the road. For a moment, they were airborne then the car dropped dramatically and slammed into something hard. Natalie's world went black.

CHAPTER 2

*D*istant crying slowly penetrated the fog enshrouding Natalie's mind. Something cold and wet dripped in her eyes.

"What the hell?" she muttered groggily. Where was she? Why was it dark? And wet?

The wailing persisted, and she swiped vainly at the moisture on her face, wishing the ringing in her ears would ease.

Slowly, things came back to her. The darkening night, the rain, the swerving pickup headed toward her.

Mathew!

Her heart stopped for a second before exploding into double-time beating.

"Shh, baby." She tried to ease his frantic cries. Her vision swam in and out of focus, and her head ached abominably. Agonizing pain throbbed beneath her seatbelt. She unbuckled, and the pressure eased a little. Bruises were already forming. She turned toward Mathew. Pain swamped her, and her stomach lurched. *Concussion*, a distant part of her mind informed her as she swallowed hard, hoping to keep nausea at bay.

"Suck it up, Walker. You don't have time to be sick." Moving slowly, she reached out toward Mathew.

"It's okay, baby. Mommy's here." She blinked rapidly to clear the water from her eyes. Damned rain was getting into the car. The near dark made it almost impossible to see, so she felt her son's limbs for damage. Her touch and soft words seemed to calm him, and his frantic cries turned to soft hiccups of distress. She stroked his head and face. He seemed unhurt, but it was impossible to be sure in the dark.

"Mommy?" The fear and confusion in his voice broke Natalie's heart.

"I hurts, Mommy," he sobbed.

"I know, Mathew. Mommy hurts, too. It'll all be better soon."

Don't panic. Get out of the car and take care of him. The small logical part of her brain rattled off instructions and kept total panic at bay.

"Light. I need more light." She turned and fumbled for the strap on Mathew's car seat. Turning the seat sideways, she checked him over as well as she could in the dim light cast by the headlights and the soft glow of the dashboard.

"Hi, Mr. Mathew." She touched him gently. "Guess we're in a pickle now. I'm thinking that since the car isn't running, it's probably broken." She kept her voice calm and soothing while she vented her fears aloud. She unfastened his car seat buckles. "Sit still for a minute. Mommy needs to think."

"Well, I guess we don't have much choice. We'll climb the hill to the road and try to catch a ride to town. We'll get wet, but we'll be fine."

"I don't wanna get wet."

"Think of it like playing in puddles. You love stomping in the muck." *Lord, let us get out of this without too much trouble.*

"Daddy won't like it."

"Lucky for you, Daddy's not here. We can get as muddy as we want."

"Yay." He clapped his hands excitedly.

Thunder boomed repeatedly, and lightning illuminated the sky. "Boy, the storm sure is noisy, isn't it?" At three, Mathew wasn't skittish, but Natalie kept up a steady stream of encouraging chatter to help him stay calm. The bright flashing made it easier to find their coats in the darkening gloom. Moving quickly but carefully, she slipped her son into his jacket and shoes then struggled into her jacket.

"Mommy's heels are going to make this walk difficult." Silently, she chastised herself for not changing out of her expensive dress and into something more practical. What kind of an idiot ran away in a thousand-dollar cocktail dress and Christian Louboutin heels? "I don't think I should be digging in the trunk for bags right now. It's raining too hard. Hang on for two shakes."

She opened her door and stepped out cautiously. Waiting for the next flash of lightning, she looked around. Her car was wedged against a large boulder at the base of a steep incline. The climb wouldn't be easy, especially not while helping Mathew.

She reached into the car and helped him climb out.

"There's a big hill here. You'll have to walk until we get to the top." She hefted him up and hugged him close. "There's Mommy's big boy. Are you okay?"

He nodded uncertainly, and she draped her purse diagonally across her body and gave him a kiss. "I know you hurt, and Mommy knows it's dark and scary and rainy. We'll be inside again soon." She set him down and grasped his hand. "Here we go, buddy. We're going to climb this big old hill and see what's up top."

"It's dark." He clutched her hand tightly. "Carry me?"

"I'm afraid not, Mathew. You're a big boy. You can do this."

"'Kay."

His obvious reluctance made her smile. One of the best things about her son was that he seemed to know when to listen. He didn't obey her all the time, by any stretch of the imagination, and she was glad he chose to listen now.

Every inch of her body ached and complained as they made their slow, painful way up the steep incline, stopping every few moments to rest. Natalie made pointless small talk, her nervous chatter helping to block the rising tension and panic that threatened to choke her. They struggled their way upward, at times slipping and falling. Once, they slid backward until they bumped into a tree that halted their downward progress. The thin strap of her shoe snapped, her foot lurched to the side and the shoe was gone. Rocks and sharp sticks bit into the bottom of her foot, but she barely noticed. With the next lightning flash, she was discouraged to discover they'd only covered a quarter of the distance to the top. Would they ever make it?

"Hello down there." A masculine voice called from above and a light flashed in her eyes.

"Help us!" she shouted, flinging her hand up to block the light. "You're blinding me." Tears of relief slid down her face, mingling with the rain. A tiny voice in the back of her mind warned that this stranger might be one of Stanley's goons, but she ignored it. She and Mathew had to get out of this valley and find someplace dry. She'd worry about Stanley after Mathew was out of the weather.

"Stay still," the deep, masculine voice called back. "Let me grab a rope. It's too slippery to come down without one." The light disappeared, and the night rushed back, darker than ever.

"Hey, muffin," she knelt and hugged Mathew close. "That man is going to help us up the hill."

Mathew snuggled into her embrace, his tiny body shivering.

"Oh, baby, you're freezing. I'll bet this nice man has a heater in his car. We'll be warm in no time." She pulled off her jacket and wrapped it tightly around her son. Rain soaked through her thin cotton cardigan in seconds.

The light of a flashlight bobbed down the hill toward them. Lightning flashed, illuminating a man in sturdy work clothes. He looked vaguely familiar, but he didn't have the air of one of Stanley's goons.

She had no choice. She had to trust him, at least long enough to get up the hill.

"Anyone else in the car?"

Natalie shook her head.

"Can you walk?"

"Yes." Relief and fear laced her voice now that salvation was at hand.

"Grab the rope behind me, and pull yourself up the hill. I'm going to pick up the child and carry him."

"M-Mathew," she stammered, her teeth chattering.

The man knelt in front of them and looked Mathew in the eyes. "Hey there, young fella. My name is Clint. I'm going to help you up this big hill. Is that okay?"

Mathew looked toward Natalie, shying away from the stranger.

"It's okay, baby. Go with the man. Mommy's coming right behind."

Mathew gave her another questioning, nervous look, and she nodded.

"Go with him."

Mathew was normally reticent and shy of strangers, so she was surprised when he obediently climbed into the man's arms but kept his eyes on Natalie for reassurance.

"Up we go." Clint snuggled Mathew in his arms. "Good man. I know it's wet and dark out here, but I'll have you and your mom safe in no time." He cast a quick glance at Natalie. "Follow us." He started picking his way carefully up the slope. Mathew kept his gaze on Natalie over Clint's shoulder.

Natalie's relief at their rescue battled fear this man might know her husband.

"Don't be an idiot. It hasn't even been twenty-four hours since we left home. He can't have found us yet," she mumbled. Putting one foot slowly in front of the other, she followed Clint up the hill.

"Did you say something?" Clint asked over his shoulder.

"No. I'm coming."

As she climbed, the ground grew increasingly slippery, and she had to rely more and more on the rope and her tired arms for support. Her head ached, and her vision swam, but she carried on, not stopping when she lost her second shoe. She had to keep moving, for Mathew. She wanted to be out of this valley and back on dry ground.

The wind blew a gust of rain into her face. Okay, maybe not dry ground but at least, flat ground. Exhaustion dragged at her feet, but she reached the crest of the hill and dropped down. Gravel dug painfully into her knees, but she didn't care.

"Mommy?" Mathew's plaintive query jerked her to her feet.

"Coming, baby." She lifted her head. There was a tow truck parked thirty feet away, on the side of the road, its lights flashing.

"Come on, ma'am. Let's get you inside, out of the rain." Clint walked to the truck and popped the passenger door open.

He set Mathew on his feet and knelt down to his level. He put one hand on his shoulder to get his full attention. "We'll have to get you out of that wet jacket. I have a nice, warm blanket inside to wrap you in. Okay?"

"'K-k-k-kay," Mathew chattered, his voice almost a whisper.

Clint boosted Mathew inside the truck, stripped him down to his underwear and wrapped him in a soft, fleecy blanket. "Now, it's Mommy's turn."

Natalie hobbled the last few steps forward and pulled her cardigan tight. "I don't need a blanket, just some heat."

"Nonsense. Take off that sweater. The heat will come through faster."

He was right.

She shrugged out of the sweater, only half-registering the mud and bloodstains on the once pristine knit fabric. He handed her a blanket and ordered her into the truck. Balling up their drenched clothing, with Mathew's shoes tucked inside, he tossed the bundle behind the seat and shut the door.

The silence from the deafening storm was a relief.

Natalie pushed her hair back from her face, leaned forward and cranked up the heat as Clint rounded the truck. Blessed hot air blasted from the dash vents and up from the floor. She pulled Mathew into her arms, rubbing him briskly to warm him. Tears streaked down her face, and for the life of her, she couldn't decide if they were tears of relief or fear.

Clint slipped out of his drenched jacket, tossed it behind the seat, climbed in beside them and pulled his door shut before turning toward her. "It's only a couple miles to town. Can you manage your seatbelts?"

Natalie nodded and buckled in Mathew and then fastened hers before pulling him tight against her side and into her embrace. A sob escaped her. She ducked her head so this stranger wouldn't see her tears.

"It's okay now. I'll come back when the rain stops and get your car. You and Mathew are safe."

Another sob slipped out.

"Sorry." Her voice shook.

Clint turned away and put the truck into gear. "It's okay. You've had a huge scare." He tuned the radio to a country station and turned it low. "Going off the road like that would be terrifying for anyone."

"How did you know we were there?"

"I got an anonymous call a car went over the edge of Clive's Corner. And when I get my hands on that bastard, he'll be lucky if I don't kick his sorry ass."

Natalie recoiled from the anger in Clint's voice. She edged toward her door, pulling Mathew with her. An image of her husband's angry face flashed through her mind, and she suppressed a shudder. Why were men so brutal?

~

CLINT LOOKED at the sodden woman huddled against the

passenger door of his truck. She shivered and clutched the boy close. Her shoulders were tense and her eyes darted around the cab, looking anywhere but at him. She was afraid. Of him! And he'd rescued them. Strange. He focused his attention on the road and spared her the occasional glance.

"Sorry, ma'am. I didn't introduce myself. Clinton Dawson, at your service. I'd shake your hand, but I'm kind of busy." He spared her a quick grin as he shifted gears. "I've met young Mathew but didn't catch your name."

"Natalie." She inched farther toward the door.

He quirked one eyebrow at her, silently asking for more. No surname? Interesting.

"Watch yourself, Natalie. If you move over any farther, you'll fall into the crack between the door and the seat." He was careful to keep his voice light and teasing. He didn't want to frighten her any more than she already was.

From the corner of his eye, he noticed her startled glance. She reminded him of a deer caught in the headlights—skittish, wary and ready to bolt. He knew that look. She'd been abused. Someone had hurt this woman. Badly. He cursed silently. Men who hit women pissed him off.

"I'm not going to hurt you. I'm going to take you into town to see Doc Hardy and then find you a place to stay the night. Tomorrow, I'll go back for your car."

Clint was pleased to see her shoulders relax a touch; though, she didn't release her death-grip on the boy. His hand itched to pat her hand comfortingly, but she was too frightened for physical contact, so he banked the urge.

"Town's just around the corner here." He flipped on his turn signal and slowed for the exit. Picking up his CB radio handset, he brought it to his mouth. "Harmony, you there?"

A moment later, the radio crackled to life. "You betcha. That you, Clinton?" Her voice was heavy with the soft tones of the deep south.

"Darn tootin', darlin'." His voice mocked the woman's accent. "Call Doc Hardy, and tell him I'm stopping by with a couple folks for him to check over. There was an accident on Clive's Corner."

"Hurt bad?"

"Nothing serious. Just some bumps I expect. Later, darlin'."

He turned and winked at Natalie. "That was Harmony Farnsworth." He dropped the accent. "She's sixty-five, if she's a day, and she's the town's biggest gossip, but she's got a heart of gold. I can always count on her standing by her radio when I need a hand. I'm surprised she isn't at the party."

"Oh," Natalie whispered, her voice so low he hardly heard it.

"I think she's from one of the southern states, the deep south. Judging by the accent, at least, but she's not telling. She moved here in sixty-two, but even after all these years in Canada, she's never lost her southern drawl. Funny thing, she has a past and won't talk about it, but ironically, she sure doesn't hesitate to meddle in everyone else's affairs."

"Oh," Natalie repeated herself. "I don't need a doctor. Just take us to a hotel."

"Nonsense. You might be fine, but Mathew needs to be looked over. Doc Hardy's nothing to be afraid of. Haven may be a darn small town in the back of beyond, but Doc's no quack. He graduated top of his class and had a large, thriving practice in Edmonton before deciding he wanted a quieter life. Doc's the best."

They pulled up in front of a large, colonial-style house behind a white picket fence. The street was jam-packed with vehicles, forcing Clint to double-park the truck. "Here comes Doc now."

His voice was calm and reassuring.

Natalie turned to look out the window. "Oh my," she whispered.

Every light in the house must have been on. Light blazed out of the windows, making the large house look homey and welcoming. A dark-haired man dressed in a bright-yellow rain slicker and rubber boots jogged toward the truck. Before she could react, he yanked open the door. If it wasn't for the seatbelt, she would have fallen out.

"Hiya," the man greeted her, bracing her shoulder to keep her inside the pickup. "Doc Hardy, here. Nice to meet you. I hear you've had an accident. Are you okay to walk? Do you need a wheelchair?"

Natalie shook her head. "I'm fine." She fumbled to release their seatbelts.

The doctor leaned past her and smiled at Mathew. "Well there, young man. It's nice to meet you. Climb on out, and we'll go inside and check you over to be sure you aren't hurt."

Mathew looked at her. "Mommy?"

"Go with the doctor, Mathew. I'll be right behind you."

Mathew stared at her, clearly unsure about going with a stranger for the second time in one already frightening night. His reluctance was obvious, but he obeyed and let the doctor scoop him up.

"It's okay. Mommy's coming, too. I'll just be a second."

"Come on, Mathew," the doctor said. "Let's get you inside, out of the rain."

With that, he turned on his heel and headed toward the house, his rain slicker flapping behind him. Mathew looked back over the doctor's shoulder, his eyes never leaving his mother, but he didn't complain.

Natalie slid out of the tow truck and landed on her feet with a wince. "Ouch." She started hobbling after them. Every inch of her body ached, she was dizzy and her feet felt as if she'd walked a mile over broken glass. There was no way in hell she'd let Mathew out of her sight, though.

"What's the matter?" Clint's voice came from close behind her.

She jumped a bit and groaned at the pain it caused when she

stumbled on her battered soles. She made her way carefully toward the house.

"Nothing. A bit sore, I guess."

"Where the hell are your shoes?"

"I think I lost them on the way up the hill. At least, I remember losing one after you showed up." She stopped walking and faced him. "Thank you for helping us, for saving Mathew and me."

Before he could answer, she turned toward the brightly lit house.

"Hang on." Clint scooped her up as if she weighed nothing. "You're in no shape to walk."

She struggled to get down, each motion making her body ache and head pound. She didn't need his help. She didn't need any man's help.

"Stop it, or I'll drop you. You're a lightweight, but even I can't hold onto a wiggling wildcat. You can have your independence back after Doc sees you."

Knowing he was right, she forced herself to relax and wrapped her arms around his neck. He hoisted her higher, and she sucked in a pained breath. She groaned low in her throat. The deep breath caused her chest to ache and her shoulders to throb. Up close, he smelled of fresh rain, wood smoke and leather. The woman in her had to admit it was a nice combination. A mental headshake chased off that errant thought. How could she be thinking like that, at a time like this?

"You must be sore. Seatbelt bite, I expect. You'll have bruises galore in the morning, if you don't already." He strode easily up the three steps onto the front porch.

The door swung open in front of them, and he twisted sideways to get them through the opening.

"Where to, Jessie?"

A red-haired young woman held the door open. She wore a pretty blue dress, and her hair was artfully, but messily, piled on top of her head.

"Through to the back of the clinic. Doc has Mathew in room one. You might as well take her there, too. She'll want to be with her son."

"Thanks." He tipped his head toward the woman as they passed her. "That's Jessie. She's the doc's nurse and assistant." Several long strides carried them past a room filled with laughing people, through the house and into the clinic.

The door to the examination room was open, and he stepped inside and set Natalie gently on a chair.

"I'll wait outside." He left the room.

"Jessie, we'll need some heated blankets to warm these folks up and some hot chocolate, I think."

"What about the party?" Jessie asked quietly.

"Send everyone home. Make my apologies. Duty calls." He didn't seem particularly concerned about his guests. The doctor gave Jessie a long look.

Jessie smiled softly, nodded and left the room, easing the door shut behind her.

"Don't chase them away for us. We can come back tomorrow." *Or never*, Natalie added silently. Doctors meant records. Records meant a chance that her husband's goons could track them.

"It's late, and some folks in this town don't know when to leave. Besides, patients come before rehearsal dinner parties. Half of Haven showed up. Now, tell me what happened." He turned to Mathew. He squatted down to Mathew's eye level. "Mathew, I'm going to look at you very carefully to be sure you aren't hurt. Okay?" He eased Mathew out of the damp blanket and began a thorough examination.

Mathew whimpered at the doctor's light touches.

Natalie stood and hobbled toward her frightened son. "It's okay." She stroked his head gently. "I'll bet you're sore and scared. I know I am. Don't worry, though. The doctor will make us both feel better."

"I sure will, and this will only take a few minutes. While I look you over, your mom is going to tell me what happened." He didn't look at Natalie, but his firm tone of voice told her he meant business.

She took a deep breath then related what had transpired. "I don't remember much. A vehicle came over the hill. A truck, I think. Its lights almost blinded me. It was all over the road. I tried to get out of the way, lost control and went over the edge." A shiver at their close call skittered down her spine.

"I think I blacked out. Maybe." She shook her head uncertainly, careful not to shake it too hard. "If I did, I don't know how long I was out. My head hurts like crazy, and I feel like I was hit by a bus." She winced at her own analogy.

"Mommy," Mathew said, whimpering and struggling to free himself from the doctor's reach.

"It'll be okay, Mathew. Does it hurt?" She smoothed his hair and kissed his forehead. "Mommy hurts, too. The doctor will make us both better."

"No signs of concussion. He'll be fine. I think he might have a few bruises from the straps of his car seat, but nothing serious. Drugstore's closed, but I'll give you something for his pain. He'll need to take it for the next day or so. Keep a close eye on him and watch for signs of concussion. Bring him back in four days for a recheck."

"I will." Natalie had no intention of being in this town long enough to come back for a follow-up visit. "Good job, Mathew. You did well for the doctor. You're a good boy. Mommy is proud of you." She hugged him close, reassuring them both.

"You are indeed a good boy," Doc Hardy agreed. "Can I give him a T.R.E.A.T?"

When Natalie nodded, he offered Mathew a sticker and a small package of gummy treats.

"Made from fruit juice. No added sugar. Now, it's Mommy's turn. Hop up beside Mathew, and we'll check you out." The doc grabbed a sheet out of the cupboard, wrapped it around Mathew and tucked it in securely.

Natalie hobbled to the front of the examination table and stepped gingerly onto the footstool so she could get on the table. With everything aching, it was all she could do to climb up. The pain in her feet was almost crippling.

The doctor gave her his full attention for a moment then strode to the door. "Jessie, we need some wet cloths in here. You'll need to help her." He turned toward Natalie. "Sorry, I didn't get your name."

"Natalie."

"You'll need to help Natalie clean up before I examine her. And hurry up with those warm blankets." He closed the door. "Dang girl is never around when I need her," he muttered under his breath.

Jessie scurried in. "Out you go, you old quack. Check on the kettle for their hot drinks, and I'll get Natalie all cleaned up. I'll call you when she's ready. Take Mathew with you."

"He stays with me." Heat rose in her face, and her mouth felt as if it were filled with dust. She swallowed to clear her throat. She wouldn't risk having Mathew out of her sight. "He's been through enough. Let him stay. He won't be any trouble."

Doc Hardy and Jessie stared at her before sharing a long look. Natalie would have sworn they were reading each other's minds.

"Out you go, Doc. We'll call you." Jessie pointed toward the door. She dropped a bundle of towels on the counter and shook open a warm blanket and replaced Mathew's sheet. "This will warm you up." She picked him up and set him on a chair where he had a good view of Natalie.

"Okay then, do you want me to stay or leave while you get undressed? I'm good either way, but you look like you'll keel over any second."

"Stay," Natalie whispered. "I don't feel so good." She gagged twice and slapped a hand over her mouth. She grabbed frantically at the small, plastic basin the nurse yanked off the shelf.

"Oh, God," Natalie whispered when she was through being sick.

"Concussion." Jessie passed her a wet cloth to clean up with. "Now, go slowly. No sudden moves." She gave Natalie a moment to collect herself. "Okay then, let's remove your pantyhose."

In a few minutes, they had her cleaned up and in a hospital gown.

"I hate to say it, but this dress is ruined." Jessie held up the mud-encrusted, ripped, cocktail dress. "And it was lovely." She ran her fingers over the delicately beaded embellishments. "Such a shame."

"Throw it away. I never want to see it again."

A soft knock sounded on the door, and soon after Doc Hardy entered the examination room. He checked Natalie over carefully. Using tweezers and a magnifying glass, he carefully cleaned the debris from her feet and then washed them thoroughly.

"How did you get the bruise on your eye? It's not from the accident. Nor are the ones on your side and arm. They're older."

"I, um, I fell."

Natalie thought she heard Jessie mutter something about landing on a fist, but it was too low for her to be certain.

"Really, I'm clumsy, that's all. Can I go now?" Panic was rising. *Don't let them ask questions. I can't handle it right now.*

"We'll need to bandage your feet. Can you manage that, Jessie?" The doctor left the room then came back a few minutes later, as Jessie was finishing the bandaging.

"All done. She's ready to roll. More or less." Jessie gave a soft chuckle.

"Okay then," the doctor said, "take it easy on those feet. They're scraped raw from walking without shoes. You'll have to watch they don't get infected. And you'll need someone to stay with you. You've got one heck of a bump on your forehead, and that concussion could be serious. I don't want you alone for at least forty-eight hours. Do you know anyone around here?"

"I don't know where here is. I think I got lost."

Jessie opened the door to leave the room. "She can't stay at Harmony's. She's booked solid this week for the wedding."

"She can stay with me," Clint called through the door.

Natalie's head jerked toward the voice. "I don't even know you."

"I have a spare room. I'm not busy." He looked her up and down. "You're definitely in no shape to be alone. If something happens to you, what would happen to Mathew?" He sounded both insistent and sympathetic.

"He's right." Doc nodded.

"Isn't there someplace else? Someone else? A woman?" Natalie tried to keep her panic from showing. "A hospital? A hotel? Can I stay with your nurse?"

"There are no hotels in Haven, just Harmony's Bed and Breakfast. The whole town is bursting at the seams for the wedding. Besides, Mathew already knows me," Clint rationalized.

Natalie's head buzzed. She had no idea what wedding they were talking about. Hell, she had no idea where she was. She'd been lost for hours before crashing the car. She dropped her head into her hands and massaged her forehead. She breathed deeply and looked from Jessie to the doc to Clint, because nothing made sense.

"I think she's best off with you, Clint." Jessie picked a piece of medical tape off the table and tossed it out. "My spare room is full anyway."

"Mine is, too. It's getting so a doctor doesn't have any space of his own. Good thing these jumbo weddings don't happen often." Doc Hardy looked at Clint. "Are you okay with looking after her? She needs someone to check on her every couple hours."

"I'm good with that. My spare room is empty. I'll take her home with me."

"Good. I'll stop by and check on her tomorrow."

The conversation swirled around Natalie until she lost her

patience.

"Shh, I'm trying to think. My head is killing me."

They quieted immediately.

"I feel like I'm going to pass out."

"You need sleep," Clint suggested. "Got any spare clothes, Jessie? She can't go in that gown."

"Just take the blanket. Her dress is ruined. Bring the blankets and gown back later. Is your truck still warm?"

"I left it running. I'll carry Natalie. Doc, you bring Mathew. I'll take them to my place for the night. You can stop by in the morning and check on them."

"I'll get your healthcare numbers and other information tomorrow when I check on you," the doctor advised. "Go with Clint. He'll watch over you for the night. You'll be safe."

Natalie tried to work up an objection, but the words wouldn't form. She had no choice but to trust these people. They'd been so kind already, and she didn't have the strength to fend for herself, let alone look after Mathew.

Rummaging around in her bag, she extracted her wallet and passed the doctor her healthcare card. Counting on his professionalism, she hoped he wouldn't mention her full name. He recorded their information and handed the card back without comment.

Clint scooped her gently into his arms and another wave of nausea washed over her. She bit it back as he carried her back to the truck.

"A wheelchair would have been fine." She didn't want to be a burden, but the warmth of his arms felt wonderful.

"Hard to get one down the front steps. I wouldn't want to pitch you out and have you land on your head." His light, teasing tone made her unease flow away.

When they reached the street, she looked around confused. "Where did all the cars go?" Six cars remained, and Clint's truck looked like he had abandoned it in the middle of the road.

"Party's over. I guess everyone went home."

CHAPTER 3

atalie woke in a soft, comfortable bed. Mathew slept beside her. Sunlight peeked through a crack in the curtains and made her head hurt.

Where the hell was she?

The events of the previous night flooded her mind. Damn. Her stomach lurched at the thought Mathew might be hurt. Easing slowly upward, she discovered she wore an oversized T-shirt.

Clint.

He'd given it to her last night before helping them into bed. She flipped the covers back and looked at her son. He wore a similar shirt and had all but wiggled his way out of it. He slept peacefully and seemed none the worse for wear after their misadventure last night.

The door creaked gently, and Natalie yanked the blankets up to cover herself.

"Hi." Clint poked his head around the door. "Good to see you're awake. I see Mathew finally went back to sleep."

"Back to sleep?"

Clint nodded and stepped into the room, carrying a tray. "He was awake for a couple hours earlier but wouldn't leave your side.

27

We had toast and juice in bed." Clint chuckled. "Well, he was in bed. I sat on the floor. Then I read to him until he fell asleep again." He set the tray on the nightstand and leaned down to smooth Mathew's hair.

"Thank you." Natalie smiled at Clint. "How long did I sleep?"

"Twelve hours straight."

She gave him a disbelieving look.

"I called Doc. He said to let you sleep as long as you needed."

"Thank you." She twisted her neck, cautiously tipping her head up and down. "I think my head is feeling better, but it still aches like hell—er, heck."

"He's asleep. You can curse." Clint laughed softly. "He won't hear you. And after what you've been through, I think you deserve it. I brought you tea and coffee. I didn't know which you'd feel like. Doc says you need some more pain meds and lots of liquid."

"Coffee, please. A bit of sugar. No drugs."

"Is there anyone you need to call? Maybe, your husband?" He gave a quick glance at her wedding ring. "Family?"

"Nobody. But thanks."

"You sure? It's not a problem."

"I'm sure." Darn, why had she snapped at him? "Sorry. I'm a bit out of sorts. There isn't anyone who'll be worried about me yet."

"If you're certain." His words held doubt. He added sugar to the mug and stirred it gently. "Let me know if you change your mind."

"I will." *When hell freezes over.* Thinking of Stanley catching up to her chilled her to the bone. She tucked the covers more firmly around herself.

"You can drop the blanket. I won't ravage you."

Natalie stared at him, startled. He winked, his expression so outrageous she knew he was joking, trying to ease the tension.

"Sorry. Old habits die hard, I guess. I'm cold."

Questions shone in his eyes. Questions she had no intention of answering. Ever.

She reached out and accepted the coffee, taking a long, slow sip. "Oh, that's good. Thank you."

The cup was warm, almost hot in her hand. But it gave her something to hold, something to still the twitchy wariness shuttling about inside her.

"Can I sit?" He pointed toward the far bottom corner of the bed.

She looked at him warily for a moment before nodding. He settled himself, careful not to disturb her comfort or wake Mathew. It was pleasant to be around a man who took her comfort into consideration. He wasn't hard to look at, either.

He was tall, lean and appeared muscular and strong. His hazel eyes sparkled in the dim light of the bedroom, and he had a dimple on his left cheek that showed when he smiled at her. Any other man sitting on the bed would have made her uncomfortable. Strangely, with him, she felt... safe. Maybe because he seemed familiar. Had she met him before? Surely, she'd remember him if she had.

His dark brown hair was short but a bit raggedy. "You need a haircut."

"Yes, I do. I never seem to have time to get away from the shop. Grooming isn't high on my priority list right now."

"Oh."

"I'm swamped with work. My best employee left for college, and those crazy rains have caused a lot of accidents. I'm not complaining, mind you. I like being busy. It makes me feel... useful, I guess."

"Last night, you said you weren't busy." She blinked rapidly, trying to bring her thoughts into focus. She massaged her forehead. She twisted on the bed, and pain lanced through her chest and abdomen. "Shi-oot. Everything hurts."

"Take these." Clint handed her two pain tablets. "You're overdue by about eight hours." He held out a glass of water.

She eyed the pills warily.

"Tylenol, from the doctor. Nothing stronger."

She took them. As much as she wanted to avoid the drugs, she knew she wouldn't function without them. "Thanks." She handed the glass back after downing half the water. "Busy? Or not?" She tried to give him a penetrating stare, but squinting made her head hurt.

"Yes, I am busy at work, but not too busy to spend a few hours helping someone. The hill's too wet to pull up your car, so the repairs will have to wait. I've got Becky manning the pumps for a few hours."

Becky? Was she his wife? "Oh no! Are we in your… your wife's bed?" She struggled to get up.

Clint stood and placed a gentle restraining hand on her shoulder. "Relax. It's my bed and I don't have a wife. Becky works for me at the garage. I slept in the other room."

"Why didn't you put us in the spare room?"

"This bed is bigger and more comfortable." His glance darted to the corner of the room.

Natalie followed his gaze to discover a large, comfortable-looking, leather recliner. "You sat in the chair all night?" Why would he do that?

To her surprise, Clint blushed. "No, I kind of fell asleep." He laughed. "I ensured you were both settled, then sleep in the spare room." He shrugged and grinned, his dimple deepening. "I slept almost six hours before I woke. I need breakfast. Are toast and eggs okay with you?"

Natalie bit back a gag.

"Okay, no eggs then." He laughed. "Whole wheat toast it is."

"Okay." She leaned back and closed her eyes. She didn't think she'd be able to stomach even toast right now, but experience had taught her she couldn't take drugs on an empty stomach.

～

CLINT LEANED against the kitchen counter. Damn. Why had he agreed to let them stay here? Surely, Doc Hardy could have found a place for them. They could have stayed at the clinic overnight. The clinic was in the back of Doc's house.

"Don't try to kid yourself." He straightened and plugged in the toaster. "You couldn't let a stranger stay in the clinic all night. Especially one with a small child. They had needed a bed. The clinic didn't have any beds, just two examination tables, and the Doc's house had been full of guests. She was lucky his guests had canceled at the last minute." Clint shook his head. He tried to ignore the memory of Natalie's soft, full curves pressed against his chest as he'd carried her into the clinic. Her legs were long and had hung enticingly from under her short dress.

He popped the bread down. What was her story? She was hurting, and it was more than bruises from the accident. She had a wariness that bothered him. Something or someone had hurt her, and he suspected it hadn't been that long ago. She was like a wildcat protecting her son. She had a black eye and several bruises on her arms, some new, some faded. He couldn't stop the thought someone had been using her for a punching bag.

His shoulders tensed, and frustration rocketed through him. Damn, why did people have to hurt each other? He had no patience for men who hurt women.

He vowed to keep Natalie and Mathew safe. Nobody would hurt them again. For a moment, his vehement defense of them startled him, but relaxation and acceptance soon followed. If his mother had taught him anything before she'd died, it was to trust his instincts about people. Right now, his instincts screamed Natalie was hurt and someone had to pay for it. Natalie needed help, needed protection, and he would provide it.

The first thing he'd do was feed her. He buttered the toast, put some jam on it, added a couple slices of cheddar cheese to the plate then returned to the bedroom.

CHAPTER 4

"Oh God." Stanley Walker rolled to his knees and tried to stand. His head hurt abominably. He was nauseous and more than a bit hung over. He touched a hand to the back of his head, and it came away sticky. He glanced at his hand. Blood. "What the hell happened to me?" Try as he might, he couldn't remember most of the previous evening. The last thing he remembered was celebrating with Natalie. The fact he was lying on the floor must be her fault.

"That bitch is going to get it this time." He struggled into a kitchen chair. "I'm done playing nice." He slammed a fist on the table, wincing when the glasses rattled.

"Good morning, Mr. Walker," an annoyingly cheerful voice called from the doorway. "Can I get you a cup of coffee?"

"You're late." He didn't bother to look at his watch.

"No, sir. It's only six-fifteen. I don't start until seven."

He ignored the smirk she gave him as she made her way to the coffeepot. He'd make her pay for her insolence. Later.

"But don't you worry none. I'll have your coffee in no time. Thank heavens for this fast-flow pot. She'll spit out black gold in seconds. We'll have you right as rain in no time. Shall I start break-fast, too? I can cook some bacon and eggs. Maybe sausages, too?"

"Shut the hell up, Annabelle." He slapped his hands over his ears, wincing at the sound of his own shouting.

"Yes, sir. Right away, sir." There was a hint of laughter in her voice, but when he glared at her, she was straight-faced and serious about carefully adding sugar to a large mug.

"Here it is, Mr. Walker." She soundlessly set the cup on the table in front of him. "Oh dear, is that blood?" She patted a napkin against the gash on the back of his head.

"Not so fucking hard."

"Should I call the doctor, sir? Head wounds can be dangerous. Best get that looked at right away. You must have slipped on that water there." She waved her hand toward a damp spot on the floor.

There was a funny lilt to her voice, but his head hurt too badly to worry about it. "Get me some pain pills, call the doctor and get Natalie."

She rattled around in the cupboard for a moment then handed him two tablets and some water. "I'll look for her."

Fifteen minutes later, she returned to the kitchen. "Sorry, sir. It looks like Mrs. Walker has gone out already."

"What the hell do you mean gone out?"

"I checked the bedroom on my way to do laundry, sir. Mathew's room is empty and so is your wife's. I guess they went for a walk or something."

He swore graphically. "Get Perkins over here. Now! Tell him I pay him big money, and he better not waste any time getting here."

"Yes, sir." Annabelle snapped to attention and scurried from the kitchen, slamming the door on her way out.

~

STANLEY PEERED toward his office door when he heard a light tapping. "What the hell took you so long?"

The doctor glanced at his watch. "It's only been twenty minutes since your maid called me. I came halfway across town."

"That bitch. She'll pay for not calling you right away. What the hell is with people these days? You can't get good help anywhere."

The doctor made short work of examining Stanley. "Nothing wrong with you except a hangover and a slight knock to the head. The scrape is hardly anything. It doesn't even need stitches." He repacked his medical bag.

"Thanks." Stanley ignored the departing doctor and shoved aside a pile of papers on his desk. It angered him he couldn't even blame his errant wife for his injury. It didn't matter; she'd pay anyway.

He barely looked up at the sound of footsteps in the doorway. The private investigator he kept on retainer entered.

"My wife has taken off. You need to find her." Stanley glared at Perkins. "She's disappeared and taken the boy with her. She fucking stole my Corvette, the good-for-nothing bitch. Why the fuck did I ever agree to marry her?"

"I'll get right on it." Perkins' beady eyes shifted back and forth around the room, rather than meeting Stanley's gaze directly.

Stanley glared at him. "I want her back here in hours. Not days. Not weeks. Hours. Do you hear me?"

"I'll start with the bank and her cell phone. She'll need money to run, and she'll have to call someone. If not, the GPS chip in her phone will tell us where she is."

"Just find her, and don't let her know you're onto her when you do." He shook his fist angrily. "Once you find her, I'll take care of her myself."

He rummaged through the drawers of his desk.

"Have you located my father's bastard?" Stanley didn't bother to look at the PI.

"No. I'm following a couple leads, but I haven't found him yet. It won't be long, sir."

"Jesus fucking Christ. What the hell am I paying you for? Get your ass in gear. Get the fuck out there and find the two of them. Keep me posted. When I get my hands on that fucking bitch, she'll regret the day she ever messed with me." He waved toward to door, and the PI hurried toward it without comment.

"What's wrong, dear?" his mother asked cheerfully from the doorway. She maneuvered her wheelchair into the office and rolled to a stop beside his desk.

"Natalie ran off."

"Oh my. That's not good."

The tone of her voice had him snapping his head round to look at her. "What do you mean by that?" He rose to pace back and forth behind his massive, marble desk.

Fucking old woman was losing her mind. He couldn't wait until she was dead. It had been a relief when his interfering father had finally passed away. Now, if only he could get rid of his mother. And the bastard his father had sired. Then he wouldn't have to share the money his father had left behind. His sisters were already happily and wealthily married off, so they wouldn't get any.

"She's so ungrateful for all you give her." She gave him a wobbly smile. "You give her everything, and she doesn't care. It's good she's gone."

"She took my fucking son, and I'll have him back!"

She rolled back from the desk, appearing shocked at his vehemence. "Yes, dear. I hope you get what you deserve."

Stanley squinted at his mother. What the fuck did she mean by that? He brushed aside her comment. She was probably stoned on tranquilizers again. Maybe, one day, she'd overdose on the damned things and all the money would be his. Sure, he controlled the company and paid himself a more-than-generous salary, but he wanted it all. He deserved it all. Why the fuck did he have to share with his mother? She didn't do anything but take up space and eat.

CHAPTER 5

*D*espite her headache, boredom was setting in. Natalie scrutinized Clint's bedroom for what had to be the ninety-third time in the past four hours. Nothing had changed. It was still a clean, simple, man's bedroom. The furnishings were dark and heavy. The sheets were dark gray, and the comforter a swirl of blue tones. The leather chair in the corner appeared comfortable and inviting. Reproduction art prints by Monet and Picasso hung on the walls, and a loaded bookcase was positioned in the corner. The books called to her. She loved reading, but even with Tylenol, her head still hurt.

Mathew was starting to get fidgety.

"Mommy, I want to watch TV."

"Honey, there isn't a television in here. Play with the blocks Mr. Clint brought you." Why did a single man have building blocks? She brushed the thought aside as it was none of her business.

"I don't want to." Mathew crawled off the bed and wandered around the bedroom.

"Don't touch anything. It isn't good to touch other people's things without asking. Why don't you come back to bed, and we'll have a nap?" A good sleep would ease the pounding in her head. God, she wanted a nap, but her young son was bored and needed entertaining. "Are there any children's books on the shelf?"

"No." His lower lip stuck out in a pout.

"Please, Mathew, Mommy doesn't feel well. Let's have a rest."

"How about we watch some television?" Clint stood in the doorway.

"Yes."

Mathew's excited shout made Natalie's head pound.

"Come along, Son. You too, Mom. We'll settle you on the couch in the den for some television watching and lunch."

"I thought you went to work?"

"I did, but it's still too wet to pull your car up the hill safely. I've got my staff filling in for me, so I can keep an eye on you guys." He shrugged off his work as if it were nothing.

"You said this morning you were swamped." First he claimed he had lots of time, then he was swamped, and now he was available again?

"I am busy, but not too busy to help out a friend."

"I would hardly call me a friend. You don't even know me."

He looked her up and down, his gaze traveling from the top of her head to the tips of her toes, where they were well buried under the blankets of his bed. His eyes sparkled. What was he seeing that made him smile?

"My mom always said a stranger is just a friend I haven't met yet. And, I know this, you're a good mother to Mathew. You're scared of something or someone. And you need someone to look after you right now."

Panic washed through her. Surely, he wouldn't ask about her past. She needed to keep it a secret. She couldn't risk Stanley finding her.

"Relax, Natalie. Your past is your own."

Was she really that transparent? Could he read her thoughts?

"I won't ask questions, and I won't pry." He gave a small shrug that left no doubt in Natalie's mind that, despite his vow, he wanted to ask why she was running.

He offered her his hand. "We haven't been properly introduced. Hi, I'm Clint Dawson. I run the local gas station and garage. It's nice to meet you."

She couldn't quite suppress a smile as she accepted his hand. His palm was calloused against hers, and when he wrapped his fingers around her hand, warmth rushed up her arm.

"Natalie Schwartz, nice to meet you." She prayed he wouldn't find out she'd given him a fake name. Okay, not really a fake one. It was her maiden name. She felt terrible for lying to the man who'd opened his home to them, but she couldn't risk him letting her name slip to someone who might know Stanley.

She cleared her throat. "Thank you for taking us in."

"Mommy, I wanna watch TV."

Mathew's wistful wail made her jerk her hand back.

Clint grabbed a dark brown bathrobe from the back of the door. "Put this on and come downstairs. We'll have some tea and watch a bit of television before lunch." He held out his hand to Mathew. "Come along, Son. We'll let your Mommy cover up and meet us downstairs." They paused at the doorway. "Call me if you need help with the stairs."

Natalie watched them go, clutching the cozy bathrobe to her chest. It smelled like Clint—manly, citrusy and a bit woodsy. She inhaled deeply and buried her face in the soft fabric. "Call me if you need help with the stairs." She mimicked his tone. *Did she look that pathetic and weak?*

"I heard that," Clint's voice came from the hallway.

"Oops." She really needed to learn to keep her mouth shut. Wasn't this attribute one of the myriad of failings Stanley kept nagging her about? She heard his voice echoing in her head. "A lady doesn't say bitter, negative things. She listens to her husband. She's grateful for the advice she's been given." Thinking about his pedantic, dominating tone made her want to puke.

On one hand, he was right. But, on the other hand, his domineering manner was just a way to put her down and control her. She resented it. Why was it so easy for him to make her feel unworthy?

"Forget it. Forget him. I'm through with Stanley." Moving slowly, careful not to strain anything or aggravate her injuries, she slid from beneath the covers and, after a quick stop in the bathroom, snuggled into the bathrobe and made her way cautiously toward the stairs.

Her feet throbbed. Every muscle in her body ached, and her head was still woozy. She felt stretched, torn and compressed all at once. Every step burned. Every motion drove a knife of agony into her flesh. Clutching the oak banister for support, she cautiously made her way downstairs. She could hardly hobble forward, even with the thick bandages on her feet.

Holy crap. If she was this sore today, how long would it be before she could move freely enough to get back on the road? When would her car be ready? She couldn't afford to rent or buy one.

She paused to rest and regroup twice on her way downstairs. At the bottom, the quiet sound of the television met her from down the short hallway.

"Hi. I see you made it. Come join us." Clint patted the oversized couch where he sat beside Mathew, who cuddled into his side, mesmerized by the cartoon.

"I made it." She tried to keep her hard breathing undetected. The short trip had been more effort than she'd expected. Her feet must have been cut to ribbons. They burned like crazy, and walking on them was agonizing. It was funny. She didn't remember them hurting until she'd reached the safety of Clint's truck.

~

CLINT WATCHED Natalie pick her way across the room to the

pillow and blanket he'd set on the couch for her. Her face was pinched, and her pain obvious, despite the fact she tried to keep her discomfort secret. It was all he could do not to rush over, scoop her up and settle her carefully alongside her son. Somehow, he knew she was too proud to accept his assistance. Every move she made told him she was doing her best to be independent and keep her distance.

"Do you need more Tylenol?" he asked kindly.

"No, thank you. I'm fine. I took some before I came down." Her teeth were gritted as she gingerly lowered herself onto his mottled brown-and-tan couch.

"Liar." His smile eased the sting of his words. "You're in agony. Relax, Natalie. Let me help you. You've been through a lot. You don't have to be strong every second."

Her eyes shone, and for a second, he was sure he saw a tear in her eye, but she blinked and it was gone. What made her so wary, so determined to make it alone? He'd bet his gas station the bruises marring her otherwise flawless skin had something to do with it. Some of them were faded to yellow; others were bright purple and blue.

Anger at the person who'd hurt her made Clint tense. Who could hurt a woman like that? The image of her cowering in his truck last night popped up. It made him sad and angry people had to abuse each other. Carefully, he adopted a calm, easygoing face before she noticed his irritation. If she'd lived with anger and abuse, she didn't need him frightening her further.

"Mathew and I are watching cartoons. I was thinking of making some coffee. Can I get you one? And maybe, something for the pain?"

"I'd love a coffee, if it isn't too much trouble." She settled onto the corner of the couch, Mathew's hand in hers, her feet tucked under her. "You've been so kind. I hate to ask for anything more."

"What do you need?" He kept his voice carefully neutral. She appeared skittish. Kind of twitchy and uneasy.

"Um, never mind. I'm fine." She tucked the blanket around herself.

"Are you cold? Shall I start a fire?" It was sunny and humid after yesterday's rain, but if she was cold, he wouldn't hesitate to build a fire or turn up the heat.

"I don't need a fire." She blushed. "But I could use some socks. Even with the bandages, my feet are freezing."

He gave a soft laugh. "Was that so hard? Don't be afraid to ask for what you need."

He brought her the socks, and she slipped them on. "Do you think I could call my friend? I'll pay for the call."

"Don't be silly. Of course, you can. No need to pay for the call. I've got an unlimited, long-distance plan."

He went into the kitchen and returned with a cordless phone. "I'll wait in the other room. Give me a shout when you're finished."

He walked away.

Safely alone, except for Mathew who was busy playing with some cars, she dialed Belinda. The phone rang several times.

No answer. And no voicemail.

"Clint, I'm finished."

He returned to the living room and knelt by Mathew. "Did you reach your friend?"

"She didn't answer. Would it be okay if I called again later?"

"Call anyone you need to. My home is your home. For now, at least. You're my guests. Besides, Mathew and I are friends. Aren't we, buddy?" He ruffled Mathew's hair.

MATHEW LEANED INTO CLINT, and the small gesture nearly broke Natalie's heart. It was so casual and affectionate. This man, who'd known her son for less than a day, showed him more affection than his father ever had.

God, how had she been so blind to Stanley's flaws, to his coldness? Already, her son was warming up to Clint more than he had to any other man. She didn't know whether to smile or snatch up Mathew and run. This was the kind of man she should have married, one who openly and willingly welcomed them into his home and made them comfortable. Someone who was warm and compassionate. She'd heard about men like this. Hell, they made television shows about them. But her upbringing had shown her few, if any, heroes.

Her father came from a long line of wealthy people, each of whom had increased the family fortune. She didn't remember her grandparents, but her father had always been cold and distant. Nothing she'd ever done had been good enough.

The only time she'd managed to earn his praise had been when she'd agreed to marry Stanley. Too bad their marriage had been more of a business merger than anything else. Even now, almost four years after her father's death, she couldn't understand why he'd willed everything to Stanley and left her with nothing.

A soft sigh escaped.

"Are you okay? Are you hurting? Are you sure you don't need any Tylenol?"

She blinked at Clint. When had he stood? "I'm a bit achy." She forced herself to meet his gaze. He towered over her, arms crossed, one eyebrow raised, doubt clear in his expression. God, he looked so familiar. Something about him reminded her of someone…

"Natalie…" The single word contained both compassion and a warning.

"I'm okay. Just stressed and overtired. Yes, I hurt, but it isn't anything I can't survive. Didn't you offer me coffee?"

"Nice change of subject." He smirked. "I'm going to have a sandwich. Do you want one, too?"

Mathew leaped up and down on the couch. "Peanut butter and jelly?"

"Sure. But you have to help make them." Clint gave Natalie a quick look. "If it's okay with your mom?"

"Can I? Can I?" Mathew bounced even harder, seemingly oblivious to his injuries.

"Whoa, sport. No jumping on the furniture. You don't want to fall and hurt yourself. And don't forget, Mommy got hurt yesterday. We need to be careful around her." He scooped Mathew up, then set him on the floor. "What do you say, Mom? Can he help with lunch?"

"Are you sure he won't be a bother?"

"We'll be great. I could use a hand. Let's make some lunch."

"Go ahead, Mathew. But be good for Mr. Clint." They walked, hand-in-hand, from the room. Guilt at abandoning her son with a virtual stranger battled relief at a few moments of time alone. She closed her eyes to enjoy the relative solitude.

Was she a bad mother? She'd taken her son and run, then crashed the car, risking both their lives. Now, she was leaving him in the care of a man she'd only known for a few hours.

He might be a stranger in their lives, but he'd already shown Mathew more caring and compassion than Stanley ever had. Besides, would the local doctor send her home in the care of someone he didn't trust? It seemed unlikely. Remorse for deserting her son and for not trusting Clint battered her. She'd go help with lunch, as soon as she rested for a few minutes.

The next thing she knew, a whispering voice penetrated the sleepy fog clouding her brain.

"Set it on the table. We won't wake Mommy up to eat. You and I will park here on the floor and have lunch. We'll make sure she eats when she wakes up."

"'Kay." Mathew's whisper was as loud as his normal voice.

She couldn't stop the grin from forming.

Small fingers pried her eyes open. "Are you awake? I sawed you smile."

She loved seeing that happy smile.

"I am awake. I see you brought me a sandwich. Thank you." She bit back a laugh at the sight of the mangled sandwich on her plate. Obviously, Clint had let Mathew make it. "Did you make my sandwich? It looks delicious."

"Mr. Clint letted me make it and cut it." His eyes grew wide. "And we get chips," Mathew added excitedly. "Mr. Clint says sometimes it's okay to have chips for lunch. But not always." He frowned then smiled again. "Today, we get chips." He giggled.

"And coffee. I'll set it here on the side table for you. Give your mom her lunch and then sit down at the coffee table, and I'll bring out our plates."

Mathew pushed the food into her hands and plopped down onto his bottom immediately.

"Thank you, gentlemen. I appreciate you making me lunch."

Clint came with two more sandwiches and two glasses of milk on a tray. They ate in companionable silence for a short time. Then, his stomach apparently full, Mathew started to chatter, most of his sentences ended with, "Right, Mr. Clint?"

It hadn't even been twenty-four hours, and already her son had a bad case of hero-worship for the handsome stranger who'd invited them into his home. She had to get him away from here before he formed an attachment to Clint.

"When will my car be ready?"

"With luck, and if the rain holds off, I'll be able to pull it up tomorrow. Then I'll have to see what she needs for repairs before I know how long it'll take."

"Oh." She hadn't thought about repairs. The towing bill alone would deplete her funds drastically, and she had no idea how she'd pay to have the car fixed. Maybe, she could catch a ride to the next town. "But we need to get going."

He gave her a long, assessing look, and she prayed he didn't see the fear in her eyes. She definitely couldn't hang around this place for too long.

"I gave the car a quick once over early this morning. It definitely needs body work and a new bumper. I'm sure it'll need mechanical parts, as well. It might take some time to get parts for a classic like that. You're welcome to stay here until I get it fixed up."

"That's kind of you, but we need to go. We'll catch a bus. Or something."

"Relax, Natalie. You can barely stand on your feet and there's no rush for you to leave. Take time to heal. You're safe here."

She thought about his words and nodded. Maybe, they could stay awhile.

CHAPTER 6

Clint enjoyed his time with talkative Mathew and his beautiful mother. They turned what might have been a boring meal alone or a hasty sandwich grabbed at lunch into a delight. The three-year-old had a unique way of looking at life in a fresh light that tickled the funny bone. Natalie was pleasant and enchanting, despite the shadows lingering in her eyes.

Mathew's attention skipped from one topic to the next. Clint and Natalie shared smiles over Mathew's head as he chattered away. Each time they smiled, there was a tug on his heart. He wanted to take her in his arms and hold her close.

The sun glinted off her wedding rings, reminding him Natalie was already taken. He needed a moment away from her enticing presence. Clint stacked their dishes and carried them to the kitchen. He was attracted to her, but he was bothered by her skittishness and reluctance to accept his help.

He thought back to the previous evening and the expensive dress she'd been wearing. He didn't know much about women's fashion, but he knew quality when he saw it. Her cardigan had been Dior, and even he recognized that as a high-end name. Then there was the 1957 Corvette she drove and those glittering diamond rings. It all added up to money. Big money. He'd worked hard all his life and didn't have much use for the idle rich.

Funny thing was, she didn't strike him as the rich, helpless type. She was obviously a caring and compassionate mother. She seemed grateful for his help, too, though, still wary and protective of Mathew.

When he factored in her reluctance to call anyone and tell them she was okay, her obvious fear of him last night and the bruises that covered her arms and cheek, it was obvious she was running— probably from someone with money.

Yes, Natalie Schwartz, with her luscious curves, shapely legs and haunted blue eyes was an enigma. She was a mystery he had every intention of puzzling out. Maybe, he could convince her to stay in Haven. This idea startled him. He wasn't looking for a woman. Was he?

Easing the dishwasher door shut, he was struck by the thought his mom would have liked Natalie and she would have wanted him to help her. His mother, Nancy Dawson, had been a lot like his reluctant houseguest. They were both loving mothers with a kind, self-effacing manner.

His mother had been strong, but it must have been tough to raise Clint as a single mother, without a man's help or financial support. They'd known some tough times, but they had enjoyed more good times and been happy.

He hadn't known his father until about ten years ago. Until Nancy had passed on, Clint had believed his father dead. As he'd sorted through her things, Clint had discovered a letter she'd left behind. The missive explained how she'd fallen for a wealthy customer who'd frequented the high-end restaurant where she'd been a waitress. They'd enjoyed a few months of passion and what she'd thought was love. When she'd shared the joy of her pregnancy with her lover, he'd been less than impressed. The letter went on to say her announcement had been met with scorn. His "father" had informed Clint's mother that he was already married and made it abundantly clear he had no further interest in her or her unborn child. He'd handed her a wad of cash and dumped her, leaving her heartbroken, pregnant and alone.

His mother's letter still angered Clint. It painted an ugly image of his sire, and the reality hadn't been much better. It had been a long, slow process, but once his mother's affairs had been tidied up, Clint had searched out his father. He was pretentious, arrogant, domineering and an all-around asshole. He ruled over his wife and children with an iron hand, accepted no excuses when they failed to live up to his expectations and verbally abused them at every turn.

Clint had done his best to get along with his newfound family, but his half-brother was as nasty as his father, and his two sisters were quiet and submissive.

His birth-father's wife had been passive and subdued, but she had welcomed Clint into her home graciously. She hadn't held him responsible for his bastard status. Thinking of the kindness she'd shown him reminded him people could be generous in difficult situations.

Remembering his mother and stepmother fueled his protective urge and made him even more determined to assist Natalie. For the sake of those two women, he vowed he *would* keep Natalie safe from whatever demons chased her.

The difficult part, he decided, while washing down the counters, would be getting her to open up to him. Maybe, he could delay acquiring the parts for her car, forcing her to stay in town longer. He dismissed the idea at once. It smacked of dishonesty and deceit. He couldn't do that. It wasn't who he was.

But another idea popped into his head. Maybe, just maybe, there was another way to keep her around.

～

NATALIE LEANED against the armrest of the couch with her legs curled up beside her. Mathew slept cuddled in the crook formed by her bent legs, undisturbed by the quiet clinking of dishes and hiss of running water coming from the kitchen. After a busy lunch, Mathew had finally succumbed to his discomfort from the accident and fallen asleep. Natalie was exhausted, but her mind was going a thousand miles an hour.

She'd made a major mistake plotting her escape. She really hadn't put much thought into anything besides getting away. She didn't have enough money. She didn't have a place to go. Sure, her friend Belinda knew they were coming. But they hadn't set a time or a date. They'd just shared some emails about a visit sometime in the future. Crashing her car outside of some teeny tiny town in the middle of Nowhere, Alberta, was definitely not in the plans. She would call Belinda again. Maybe, Belinda could come get them.

Realistically, paying for car repairs was out of the question. Hell, she couldn't afford the towing bill. If she didn't need her luggage retrieved from the trunk, she'd forget the car altogether. She didn't have any options. As soon as she could walk easily, she'd take Mathew and get out of town. It'd be foolhardy to linger longer than necessary and risk Stanley finding her. She'd leave the car behind.

Would Clint get the bags and forget the car? Somehow, she doubted it.

The idea of cutting and running without explanation made her uncomfortable, but she couldn't fathom any other options. Maybe, Clint could sell it for parts or something to pay for his troubles.

No, that wouldn't work. He couldn't sell it without the registration paperwork, and that might bring her back onto Stanley's radar. She stifled the little voice that reminded her that if Clint discovered her real name, he'd know she had lied to him. There was no explaining the deception without giving up details about a past she wanted hidden.

Why did things have to be so complicated? She should have gone with her instincts and refused to marry Stanley, even if it meant her father died unhappy. Heaven knows, neither man had ever done anything to make *her* happy. She sighed heavily.

"That was a big sigh." Clint came back into the room. "It sounds like the weight of the world is on your shoulders."

"I…um…" She shrugged. "Never mind. It's hard to explain."

"Try me. I'm not just cute, you know. I've been told I'm a good listener." He gave her an outrageous wink.

She was tempted, very tempted, to give in and confide in him. She liked the compassion and encouragement in his eyes.

"I don't have any money to pay for the car repairs." The words were out before she'd even realized she was going to speak. Her hands fluttered nervously, and she forced them to relax so she didn't betray her emotional state.

"And?" His raised eyebrow indicated he knew there was more.

"I don't know how to pay you for the car, for letting us stay here, for anything. You've let us into your house, you've watched my son, you've fed us, and I can't pay you back." She swallowed hard, refusing to give in to the worry that nagged at her and made her voice tremble. She wouldn't show how vulnerable she felt.

"There's more to it than that." He stood there, looking at her, one eyebrow raised, his hands hanging at his sides. He looked relaxed at first glance.

She scrutinized his posture and saw the tension in his thighs and shoulders. Damn. She could almost feel his curiosity and suspected he wanted to hear more and was trying not to pressure her.

"I don't want to talk about it. I can't talk about it." She winced at the small untruth. "I just need to get back on the road." With Stanley's temper, her life might depend on it. She had to stay safe, to protect her son. Her body tensed, and she forced herself to let the tension dissipate.

He looked thoughtful for a moment. "You said there was no one to call, that no one was waiting for you. Why the hurry? You can't walk, you're bruised and you're battered. Take some time to heal before you run off. I understand if you don't want to share your troubles, but don't feel you have to leave this minute. You aren't ready."

"I have to go."

The kindness in his voice, the compassion, made her want to stay. She felt safe here. She wanted to curl up in his arms and give in to the sanctuary he offered. She wanted to press her lips to his and see if they were as delicious as they seemed.

Whoa, girl. Don't go there. The last thing I need is a man. My life is messed up badly enough as it is.

"Take some time to heal your injuries before you leave. You don't want to risk getting an infection in those cuts on your feet, and that concussion is no minor matter. Look, Haven's a small place. We don't get many outsiders. Nobody will find you here."

"I'm not hiding." She couldn't look at him; he might see the lie in her eyes. She hated she was turning into a dishonest person, but she had to protect Mathew at all costs.

"I'm not asking questions or searching for explanations. Your past is your business and none of mine. I'm just offering you a place to rest and heal before you leave. You can't risk Mathew getting hurt if you have trouble because of your injuries. Stay here awhile. When you feel better, you can go."

"I can't stay. We've disrupted your life enough. I already owe you money I can never repay. I can't inconvenience you any longer. We're messing up your home, disrupting your schedule and eating your food. You need your house back. I'll get out of your hair."

His hair. She wanted to touch his hair, to test its softness against her fingertips and touch his skin and feel its warmth against hers.

"You aren't in my hair."

"We're wasting your time. We're unwanted guests, and we're keeping you from your work. That's the definition of being in your hair. Is there a hotel here?"

"Natalie, you said you can't afford car repairs. How can you afford a hotel?"

"I can't, but I don't want to keep imposing on you." She hated being an imposition, even though he hadn't complained even once about them being in his home and screwing up his life.

"Can you sew?"

"What?" The sudden change of topic left her confused.

"Can you sew?"

"Yes, a bit." She didn't know what he was getting at. Belinda had taught Natalie a bit of mending at college, and she could sew a bit if she had to. She wasn't up to making a dress, but she could handle simple repairs.

"I have a suggestion. Hear me out, and don't answer until I finish laying it out. Okay?" He perched on the edge of the coffee table, his legs only inches from hers.

"Okay."

He leaned forward, elbows resting on his knees, and studied her. The thoughtful look on his face told her he was choosing his words carefully.

"I have a small house trailer behind the service station. It was my home before I bought this house, and nobody lives there now. You can stay there, and you can do my mending to pay for the rent. You can look after yourself and Mathew there, until you're feeling stronger. It will give you some independence, and I'll get my mending done." He flashed a self-pleased smile. "Do you have money for food?"

"I have enough to feed us, yes." Why did he have to hit right on the issues that plagued her most?

"So, we'll move you into my trailer. I'll get your bags when I haul up your car. You can do my mending to pay your rent."

"And your laundry." She caught the smile he tried to hide.

"You don't have to do that. I can handle my own laundry."

"Please." Couldn't he understand she needed to earn her keep?

"Natalie, I don't mind."

"Okay. We'll stay in your trailer until I feel better, but I still don't know how I'll pay for the car."

"I'm not worried about that." He shrugged. "We all have tough times. I'll fix the car, and if you can't pay me, maybe, you can find a way to help someone else later on. A random act of kindness thing. We can make the world a better place by lending someone in need a hand."

It didn't feel quite right. It was as if she were using him. But for the life of her, she couldn't think of another way out of her dilemma. What was his angle? Everyone had an angle. People didn't just help out without reason. Did they?

It wasn't as if she had a lot of options.

She reached out and grasped his hand to seal the deal. He cupped her hand, holding it gently between his. His palm and fingers were calloused and rough against hers. When he didn't let go immediately, she looked at him. His eyes sparkled, and a slim smile curved his full lips. He seemed infinitely kissable; Natalie's breath caught in her throat. If she leaned forward, just a little, she could reach his lips.

CHAPTER 7

Stanley rolled over in the luxurious, four-poster bed and looked at Alisha lying beside him. "Not bad."

"Not bad?" The petite blonde smiled at him. "I thought it was pretty damned good." She trailed her fingertips slowly down his chest. His skin was like satin. She'd never understood why he waxed his chest. He wasn't a competitive swimmer anymore. Hell, he was almost thirty-six years old and the man and looked every bit his age and more.

They'd been dating off and on for three years, and each year, he got softer and gained more weight. He was getting a paunch. He really should workout more before he had a heart attack or stroke. His size didn't matter to her. What she was really interested in was his money, the security he offered. Once, she thought he'd be her savior, her way to a better life, those days had passed.

"Shall I try again?" She kissed him deeply.

"Don't bother." He got out of her bed and headed to the en suite bathroom. "You really need to clean this place up." He waved at the clothing littering every available surface.

"You could always hire a cleaning lady for me." She was getting tired of his superior attitude. If only he wasn't so stinking rich, but money was a powerful aphrodisiac, and she wanted more. She wanted every dollar she could extract from him.

"Why the fuck would I hire a cleaning lady for you?" He glared at her. "I already pay your rent and buy your clothes. Jesus, Alisha, you're my receptionist, not my fucking wife."

God, he made her so angry. One day, she'd show him. She rolled back on the bed, angling her body toward him, hoping to entice him back to her. "Come back to bed, Stanley. I need you." She pursed her lips seductively and looked at him from beneath lowered eyelids. "Please." She drew the word into three long, sexy syllables. It was all she could do to bite back her smile when his eyes widened with desire.

Her mother had been right. So very, very right. Men were weak. They were nothing but tools, the means to an end, and she had every intention of ending this relationship holding fistfuls of his money. God, the thought of all that cash aroused her. Her hips undulated on the bed as she considered what she could do to get her hands on his wealth.

"I should go. I have a meeting in an hour."

"Come on, sexy. Just a quickie? Let me worship you with my mouth." Her tongue flicked out and wet her lips.

He didn't look as if he wanted to leave.

She rose to her knees. "Come here, Stanley. I need you." She used her throaty, enticing voice that had taken hours of practice to get just right.

He stared at her. God, men were so predictable, so easy. Flash a little skin and play the sex kitten, and they were yours. Easy, like shooting fish in a barrel. She almost laughed aloud.

Sinuously, she curled around the bed post and slipped toward the floor. She couldn't quite recall who'd said being a stripper for a few months was beneath her, but they were wrong. She had picked up a lot of alluring skills.

She stood and strolled over to him, swaying her hips enticingly.

He smelled of sweat and sex. The combination nearly made her gag. Swallowing harshly, she went to work. It didn't take long. It never did. Stanley Walker had a sensitive trigger.

She gave him a sweet smile. "Mmm, so good."

"You're a naughty bitch. I wish my frigid wife could fuck like you."

"You could divorce her." Alisha rose slowly to her feet. "You know I'd step in and take care of your needs."

"The last thing I need is another woman." He backed away. "Besides, I can't fucking divorce her. I don't know where the hell she is."

"Probably at home with your brat." Her words were deliberately dismissive. She hated when he rattled on about his home life.

"She fucking ran off, but I'll find her, so shut your damned mouth." Turning on his heel, he stomped into the bathroom and slammed the door.

Alisha stared at the closed door, tapping one finger against her front tooth. So, his wife had run off. This could be an opportunity for her. If she played her cards right, maybe, she could convince him to divorce his wife and marry her. Then, after a couple months of living with him, she could divorce him and take her share of the money.

Yes, this could be good.

She rose gracefully to her feet, slipped into a silk bathrobe and began plotting her strategy.

Put on your happy face. She smiled at her reflection in the dresser mirror. *You can do this. You've already invested three years in him. A little more time won't hurt. Make yourself pretty and go after him.*

She ran a brush through her hair, applied some lip gloss, then slipped into the bathroom as Stanley was shutting off the shower.

"Hey, sexy." She reached out and grabbed a towel from the shelf. "Let me dry you off so you can get back to the office." She chattered away, talking of inane things like the weather until he was dry. She kissed him deeply, moaning with mock desire. "I wish you had more time. I love being with you. I need you again." The words were a lie, but after years of watching her mother lie to her Johns, Alisha had learned more than a few ways to intrigue a man.

By the time Stanley was dressed and out the door, she'd extracted a promise to take her out to dinner at a private club the next evening.

"Let the seduction begin." She leaned against the closed door and laughed.

Soon, very soon, he'd be eating out of her hand and she'd be living with him.

She refused to acknowledge how her mother, once a high-end escort, had ended her life as a broken-down streetwalker. Her mother had shed every aspect of morality in her search for the right man to support her expensive tastes. She had even sold Alisha's virginity to a favorite client on her daughter's fourteenth birthday.

For the life of her, Alisha couldn't decide if she hated her mother for taking her down this road or if she recognized her determination to do anything to achieve her goals.

CHAPTER 8

Natalie's feet still hurt, but not as bad as they had yesterday or the day before.

She stood at the stove, stirring her signature spaghetti sauce. The spicy aroma of basil, garlic, onion and red and green peppers permeated the kitchen. Their tang mingled nicely with the smell of fried ground chicken and tomato sauce simmering inside another pot. Natalie carefully added the contents of the frying pan into the bubbling pot of tomato sauce, tasted the mixture, then added some salt and a teaspoon of sugar. Her signature pasta sauce was finished. A few more minutes and it'd be perfect to pour over the spaghetti that bubbled in another pot.

She loved to cook. It had been a rare treat to spend time in the kitchen when she'd been with Stanley. Sharing an apartment with Belinda during college had opened Natalie's eyes to the pleasure and relaxation to be found in the kitchen. When they'd met, Natalie couldn't even boil an egg. She smiled at the memory. They'd spent hours together, cooking, laughing and learning. Eventually, she'd refined her skills and become a decent cook. She wasn't a chef by any stretch of the imagination, but she could hold her own in the kitchen.

"Mommy, when is Mr. Clint coming home?"

"I don't know, sweetheart. He had to go to work."

When Clint had left earlier, he'd told them he had to stop by the garage. He hadn't mentioned how long he'd be gone or when he'd be back. Natalie hadn't questioned him; it wasn't her place to intrude on his life any more than she already had. Hours had passed, with time ticking by at a snail's pace. The afternoon dragged on and on. Mathew had slept for a short time, but it was getting late, and he was hungry and starting to get grumpy. He wasn't used to staying up late. He was an early riser and went to bed in the early evening.

Natalie started their dinner having given up on waiting for Clint to return home. She liked his kitchen. Although it wasn't big, it was bright. The falling sun didn't diminish its space. Light streamed through the large windows, reflecting off the stainless-steel appliances and shining countertops. The walls were light tan, the cupboards white and spotless. It was one of the cleanest kitchens she'd ever been in. A heavy wooden table with four matching chairs had seen a lot of wear. The placemats, oven mitts and tea towels were decorated with bright, bold geometric designs that echoed the pattern in the framed prints hanging on the wall behind the table. It was a bit masculine, but homey and welcoming.

She grabbed the tall stool from the corner, pulled it up close to the stove and perched on it, gently stirring the pasta to keep it from sticking. She glanced at Mathew, who sat on a small navy and green throw rug in the corner of the kitchen, playing with a box of cars that Clint had found earlier.

He looked at her. "But I misses him."

"I'm sure he'll be home soon." She hoped she wasn't fibbing. She'd understand if Clint had chosen to escape for a few hours. In addition to having a business to run, he'd been cooped up in the house with them for days. For a man who claimed he was short-staffed at work, he sure spent a lot of time at home.

"Supper will be ready in a few minutes. Go wash up, and then you can help me set the table."

"But I don't know how to setted the table."

"Neither do I." Clint's voice came from the hallway. "But we can figure it out together."

"Mr. Clint, you came back." Mathew leapt to his feet. "I thought you forgetted us."

Clint stooped down to Mathew's level. "I could never forget someone as special as you and your mom." Clint patted him on the shoulder. He winked at Natalie over Mathew's head and gave her a soft smile, a dimple appearing in his left cheek.

Natalie's heart stopped and burst into overtime beating. Heat rushed to her face. The man was too damned handsome for his own good.

"Supper's almost ready." She turned away to hide the blush she felt staining her face.

"So I heard." He turned Mathew toward the hallway. "Go get washed up, Sport. I'll be right there."

Mathew scampered out of the kitchen.

"You didn't have to make dinner. I was planning on cooking when I got home." He stepped into her line of vision.

"Sorry." She dipped her head apologetically.

Clint gave her a long, hard look, and she turned her attention back to the stove.

"Why do you do that?"

"Do what?"

"Apologize for nothing." He caught her gaze.

"Sorry." She twitched like a bug under a microscope, discomfited by his accurate statement.

"See, you're doing it again. You haven't done anything to apologize for."

"Sorry. Dang. Never mind. Go get washed up." She waved her wooden spoon toward the door.

"You're not getting off that easily." He winked.

"Go." She shook the spoon at him.

"Yes, ma'am. Right away, ma'am." He bowed low and backed toward the door. "Don't hit me, ma'am." He peeked at her and winked again. "We'll be back in a flash, all spit-polished and shined up."

The man had an uncanny way of picking up things she wanted hidden. It was as if he could see her thoughts. She had to watch herself. Worse than that was his habit of winking and catching her gaze. A girl could get used to having a man flirt like that.

She took a deep breath. *Brace yourself, Nat. Your presence here is only temporary. You'll be gone before you know it, so don't get attached.* She hobbled around the kitchen, pulling out dishes and ladling the pasta and sauce into serving bowls.

"You should be sitting. Doc said to rest."

"Mathew needs to eat before his bath." She limped toward the table.

"Another two minutes won't hurt him. Sit. Mathew and I will set the table and serve you. You're dependent on me until those feet heal." Rummaging around in the drawer, he withdrew some silverware and napkins. "Put these on the table, Sport." He handed them to Mathew. "One each for the three of us."

Obediently, Mathew distributed the items somewhat haphazardly on the table. "Can we eat?" He climbed up onto a chair.

"Not yet. Come put these bowls on the table while I bring the food and juice over. Then we can eat."

Mathew hopped off the chair, and it teetered, almost toppling over.

"Slow down. No need to flip the furniture. A man takes care of his things, and his friend's things, too."

"'Kay." Mathew looked at his feet.

Clint set the serving bowls on the table and squatted down to Mathew's level. "Look at me, Mathew." When the boy looked up, Clint caught his gaze. "You're not in trouble. I'm just telling you it's good to be careful and to take care of things. We don't want to break something accidentally." He handed Mathew a plate. "Give this one to your mom and come get another."

Wordlessly, Natalie watched the interplay between her host and her son. Clint was gentle but firm with him, and Mathew eagerly obeyed his instructions. Together, they set the table before Mathew carefully climbed onto his seat.

"See, Mr. Clint. I climbeded up careful. I didn't bust nothing."

"I saw that. Well done. Thank you for being careful with my things." He ruffled Mathew's hair and smiled at him before he turned to Natalie. "Thank you for cooking dinner."

"You're welcome. Pass me your plate, and I'll serve." She held out her hand.

"Not tonight. Tonight, I serve. Hand me your plate. I appreciate you cooking for us, but you should have rested. Let me thank you by serving and cleaning up."

"Here's my plate, Mr. Clint." Mathew held out his plate, eagerly awaiting his supper. "I'm starved."

"Me, too, Sport. Me, too."

They all laughed together.

~

NATALIE EDGED SLOWLY into the living room after putting Mathew to bed. Her feet ached, her head pounded and the bruises covering her torso throbbed painfully. She eased herself onto the couch, leaned back, then closed her eyes and sighed in relief.

"You sound beat. Do you need something for the pain?"

"No. I'm good." She didn't want to put him to any more trouble.

"You're a fibber." His voice was mocking and vaguely accusatory.

Her eyes flew open, and her heart started pounding double time. She winced. "I am not."

"Yes, you are." He shook his head. "I can tell by watching you that you hurt like crazy. You must be in agony from the accident, and it's no easy feat to care for an active kid all day." He gave her a quizzical look.

"Oh." She relaxed a touch. He hadn't caught onto her lies about who she was. Thank God. "I do hurt a bit. But I don't want to take too many drugs."

"Doc says you need them. I think you should listen. When's the last time you took something?"

"Um. This afternoon."

"Specifically?" He quirked one eyebrow at her, clearly skeptical.

"Earlier." She leaned back, closing her eyes to avoid looking at him. She didn't want to acknowledge his concern, or his caring. She wanted—needed—to keep him at a distance until she and Mathew moved into the trailer. She had to learn to rely on herself, to be independent.

"Natalie." His voice was soft with warning.

"Fine. At noon. Twelve-fifteen to be exact." She opened her eyes.

He glanced at his watch. "It's almost nine-thirty. Take something." He suited actions to words, disappeared into the kitchen and came back with a glass of water and some Tylenol.

Reluctantly, she accepted his offering, swallowed the pills, then set the glass on a coaster. She didn't like drugs. They messed with her head and gave her strange dreams.

"Thank you." She sighed. "I wish I didn't need them. The pain is starting to get better, my feet look good, but they still hurt like hell. Er, heck."

"You'll get better every day. Maybe, by Tuesday, you'll be well enough to move into my trailer." He sat beside her, close enough his body heat radiated to her, yet not quite touching her.

"I'm sorry we're messing up your home and your life." She hated being a burden on anyone, but especially on this kind-hearted man. Did he have to sit so close? She wanted to snuggle into his warmth and rest her head on his chest.

"You aren't messing up my life or my house. I don't want you to leave, but I can tell you aren't comfortable here." He shifted, draping his arm across the back of the couch.

She clenched her hands into fists to keep from pulling his arm down against her shoulders.

He picked up the television remote then set it back down. "I know what it's like to stay somewhere you don't feel comfortable. Stop worrying about it."

"That's easy for you to say. I feel like an imposition, but I do appreciate your help." She didn't want to confess that being here, in his home, felt entirely too comfortable. She couldn't risk getting attached to him because that would lead to her lies coming out and maybe, God forbid, to Stanley being able to find her.

"Speaking of help." He grinned. "I managed to pull up your car today. She's in one hell of a mess. She needs the entire front end rebuilt, a new radiator, a fan and a fan belt, two new tires and rims and a boatload of bodywork. Getting parts won't be easy or cheap."

"Shit." She slapped a hand over her mouth. "I mean darn."

Clint laughed. "It's okay to swear, you know. It's a big chunk of news to choke down."

"That's true, but I try not to cuss because of Mathew." She shook her head. "I can't pay for all that. Can you get it on the road cheap? Skip to bodywork?"

"I'll do my best to make her roadworthy, and I'll run the costs by you before I do anything. And, since your money is tight, I'll skip the cosmetic repairs. Though, it'll break my heart to leave such a beauty with blemishes."

"Thank you." She gave in to temptation and stole a quick hug. He was warm and strong and smelled delicious. It took all her willpower to keep the hug in the quick, gratitude-hug zone. She wanted to burrow deep and draw on his strength and kindness.

She leaned back, resting her head against the couch and his arm. She looked at him. He was watching her. Did he like what he saw? Why did she care? She certainly wasn't looking for a man.

Lord knows, she was having trouble enough getting rid of the one she had. There was no sense in complicating the issue.

But darn, Clint was attractive and much kinder than the men who ran in her normal social circles. Was it small-town living that made him that way, or was it just his nature? She refused to entertain the thought he might be putting on a show. He seemed too genuine for that to be the case.

Don't fall for him. We're not staying here. As soon as my car is on the road, we're heading to Belinda's.

She'd called her university roommate and friend with Clint's cell phone to let her know about the accident. She'd asked Belinda to come get her. Unfortunately, Belinda's husband was battling end-stage cancer, and there was no way she could free herself to pick up Natalie and bring her to the ranch. That left Nat stuck in Haven until her car was repaired.

atalie moved a load of Clint's work pants from the washer to the dryer, added a fabric softener sheet, closed the door, then turned it on. Moving quietly to avoid waking Mathew, who'd fallen asleep on the living room floor, she tiptoed to the loveseat and sat. Her feet were feeling much better, as long as she didn't spend too much time standing.

It had been three weeks since the accident, and they'd been living in Clint's trailer for two weeks. Every few days, Clint stopped by to drop off laundry and to pick up what he'd left on previous visits. She was doing more laundry than she'd ever done in her life, but she didn't mind. It kept her busy.

Is he making extra laundry in an attempt to make me feel useful? He has to be. Nobody had that much laundry.

Mathew wanted to visit Clint every day, and on occasion, keeping her son distracted from his obsession with their rescuer was a full-time occupation. Clint's frequent visits weren't helping. She enjoyed his company, in spite of herself.

The trailer was small—nothing more than a holiday trailer that had been skirted in. There were two tiny bedrooms, a miniscule bathroom and a combination room that melded living room and kitchen. The washer and dryer were on an add-on porch that served as an entryway and laundry room.

The trailer's original built-in furnishings had been replaced with a kitchen table and chairs, loveseat, rocker and entertainment center. Everything was older, but clean and well cared for. Decorated in navy and gray, Natalie's temporary residence was masculine but neat, tidy and cozy. It felt like…home. It was much more a home than the luxurious monstrosity she'd shared with Stanley.

Here, Mathew had a small toy box and a shelf of books in the living area, as well as in his room. Stanley had never allowed Mathew's things outside the nursery, and her son loved the freedom to play wherever he wanted.

The trailer sat about a hundred yards behind Clint's gas station and garage, the only one in the small town of Haven. His business also boasted a diner and convenience store. Nestled in the trees, their new home had a small, fenced-in yard with a spacious deck and a gravel walkway.

Footsteps on the gravel alerted Natalie someone was coming. She peeked out the window, careful to remain unseen. Panic darted through her. *Please, please, don't let it be Stanley or one of his goons.* Her heart pounded. Dammit, she hated living in fear like this.

When Clint came into view, relief flooded through her. She breathed deeply, trying to restore her calm. As he came closer, soft sounds of feminine laughter and the tread of a second set of feet sounded. Surely, he wasn't bringing someone over unannounced. Panic surged again. She didn't want to meet anyone. Every person she came in contact with increased the chances of Stanley finding her. She had to keep herself and Mathew in seclusion until Clint finished repairing her car and they could leave Haven.

She hastened to the door and opened it before Clint could knock and wake Mathew.

"Hi."

His smile lit his face and made her feel warm all over.

"I brought you some company. I thought you guys might be getting lonely out here." He waved toward a willowy blonde standing behind him. "Natalie, this is Lisa. She works for me at the diner. And this…" He reached around Lisa and tugged a diminutive blonde girl with pigtails from behind her. "This is her daughter, Amy."

Lisa was gorgeous. She had a trim, fit figure and perky demeanor. Her hair was cropped short and spiky. She looked like a pixie. All that was missing were wings. She had a bright smile and flashing green eyes. She looked put-together, friendly and sexy.

Jealousy blazed through Natalie. Who was this woman, and why was she with Clint?

"Um, hi," Natalie stammered. "Won't you come in?"

"Where's Mathew? He usually meets me on the deck."

"Sleeping on the living room floor. He fell asleep playing with his trucks. Come in." Natalie gestured inside.

"Gracious, no. Let sleeping children lie." Lisa grinned at Natalie. "Nice to meet you. Amy, go play on the swings for a minute."

"You said there was kids." Amy pouted.

"There is." Clint picked Amy up, swung her in a circle then set her back down. "But Mathew is sleeping. We don't want to wake him up. Come on. I'll push you on the swing while your mom gets to know Miss Natalie."

Amy squealed with excitement and raced off the deck toward the swing.

"I'll make coffee and shout when it's ready."

For a moment, the two women watched Clint walk away. "That is one good man." Lisa grinned.

"He is. He's been so kind to us since the accident. Is he… Um…are you… That is… Never mind."

Lisa laughed aloud. "No, he isn't mine."

"Why not?" Natalie couldn't keep the surprise from her voice.

"Hell if I know. Lord knows, he's hot enough." Lisa waved a

hand in front of her face. "Somehow, we never hit it off that way. We're just friends."

"Just friends? I find that hard to believe." She slapped a hand over her mouth. "Sorry."

"Sad. Isn't it?" Lisa laughed again. "He hired my husband as an apprentice mechanic when we landed in town, then he gave me a job when Davin died. His kindness not only allowed me to keep our home, but also to stay in Haven. I work in the café most weekdays and have weekends off."

"Come inside." Natalie opened the door. She refused to acknowledge, even to herself, she was relieved there was nothing between Lisa and Clint. "I'll make that coffee and find some snacks for the kids. Mathew will be up before long."

She wasn't that eager to invite this stranger into her home, however temporarily it might be hers, but she owed it to Clint to be kind to his friend.

"So, what brought you to Haven?" Lisa followed her onto the porch.

"Um, I crashed my car on the way to…to someplace else."

"Someplace else? That's a bit vague." Lisa gave her a piercing look.

"It doesn't matter where. I'm only here until Clint gets my car back on the road. Then we're off." Natalie busied herself with the coffeemaker, uncomfortable with the turn of conversation.

"I'm not going to pry. Your secrets are safe with me. Clint said you needed company, I had spare time and Amy can always use a friend. So, here we are." She flipped her arms out in a take-it-or-leave-it gesture.

"Secrets? I don't have secrets." Natalie hoped her face didn't give away the lie.

"Girl, we all have secrets. Haven is, well, it's a haven for people with secrets." She laughed at her word play. "I have yet to meet anyone in this town who doesn't have a skeleton in their closet."

Natalie looked at Lisa with disbelief, then poured water into the coffeemaker.

"Yah, I wouldn't have believed it either. But when Davin and I landed here, we had secrets, too. Everyone does. Haven is the dangdest place for secrets. But, on the upside, when everyone has secrets, they don't poke their noses into your business. I guess they're afraid you'll poke back." She shrugged.

"Let's have coffee outside, in the shade." Natalie turned on the pot.

"Boy, talk about changing subjects."

"How old is Amy?" Natalie asked.

"She'll be four next week. You and Mathew will have to come to her party this weekend."

"I don't think so. We'll hang out around here while we wait for my car."

"Don't be silly. A bunch of four-year-old children don't care about who you are, right? Just show up, eat cake and hot dogs and play pin the tail on the monkey."

"On the monkey?" Natalie gave Lisa a quizzical look.

"On the monkey! Donkeys are, and I quote, 'gross.'"

They shared a laugh at the whimsies of a child's mind.

"Amy's hated them since she saw one poop at the petting zoo. You really should come. No pressure, but I cordially invite you and Mathew to Lisa's fourth birthday party. Saturday at three. The green house on Picket Drive, just down from the doctor's office. I know you know where that is. Got any cookies to go with that coffee?"

"Cookies, I have. Cream and sugar?" Natalie poured three cups of coffee and two sippy cups of juice before adding a plate of home-baked cookies to the tray.

"Black for me. Clint likes—"

"Three sugars. Ugh."

They groaned in unison as Natalie dumped sugar into one of the mugs.

"Mommy, who that?" Mathew's sleepy voice interrupted their laughter.

"Mathew, come meet Miss Lisa. She came to visit. Her daughter, Amy, is outside with Mr. Clint."

"Mr. Clint is here?" Mathew raced toward the door.

"Don't forget your shoes."

Lisa seemed a bit surprised at the speed he moved. "Wow, he gets going fast."

"He wakes up hard and goes down easy. Plays until he drops. Getting him to sleep is never an issue. If he wakes up on his own, he's great. But don't you dare wake him up before he's ready. If you do, he's impossible to deal with." Natalie shrugged.

"Amy's the opposite. She resists sleep as long as she can and always wakes up grumpy. I just throw food at her until she's happy."

Lisa's light tone eased a bit of Natalie's discomfort at having a stranger in her home. There was something nice about bonding with another mother; it wasn't something she'd done before. Stanley considered playgroups beneath his status and had forbidden Natalie from signing Mathew up for any. Few of the women in their elite social circle had young children, and those who did left the dirty job of raising children to their nannies.

She spent a few minutes with Lisa, chatting about the pleasures and pains of children. Maybe, she did need a friend. It would be nice to spend time with someone who had more on their mind than designer shoes and Coach bags.

"I'm glad Clint brought you over. It's nice to have someone to talk to." Natalie smiled. "You get the door; I'll bring this." Natalie picked up the tray.

She loved the yard. It was small, with the deck taking up about half the space. There was a bit of grass, a swing set and a sandbox. The entire area was surrounded by a white picket fence and shaded by four large trees that grew in the corners of the property. The trailer was parked on the west edge of the yard and the swings were positioned toward the east. The shade cast by the trees was a nice respite from the sun's relentless heat.

"So, how are you girls getting along?" Clint settled himself at the picnic table on the deck, after pushing the kids on the swings.

"Nat's a bit shy. I'm thinking she has some secrets."

"I do not."

"Don't we all?" Clint sipped his coffee. "Hell, Lisa was a scared pregnant, twenty-year-old when I met her. She was on the lam with Davin, hiding from her parents."

"I wasn't hiding from them. I didn't want them to know about the baby until she was born."

"And you didn't want them to know you'd run off to Vegas to marry Davin, either."

"Whatever." Lisa stuck out her tongue. "I know you have secrets. I just haven't figured them out yet." She gave him a penetrating stare. "But I will."

"No secrets here. My life is an open book." There was a look in his eye that hinted that, maybe, he wasn't telling the truth.

"Bullshit. The way I hear it, you showed up in town with nothing but the clothes on your back and took a job pumping gas. Now, you own the gas station, garage, diner and that campground." She gestured to the trees at the left of Natalie's trailer. "Just how does one manage all that in only six years?"

Natalie jumped to her feet. She didn't want to talk about secrets. She didn't want anyone prying into her life. "I'll check the kids." She hurried off the deck.

Across the small yard, she pretended she couldn't hear their whispered conversation.

"Way to go, dipshit. I told you she's running from something. You'll scare her out of town." Clint's words carried on the still air.

Lisa looked at him dumbstruck. "Oh my God, you like her."

"Keep your voice down. Of course I like her. She's a nice woman and a good mother."

"No, I mean you *like* her." She used a singsong voice and

laughed when Clint blushed. "Holy crap. I never thought I'd see the day when date-no-one Dawson found a woman. You've got it bad, my friend. Bad with a capital B." Lisa taunted him musically.

"And you have a nosy mind. Be her friend. Don't press her. Don't let on that I like her. You owe me."

His words sobered Lisa's laughter. "That I do." She shrugged. "I'll be nice, and I won't pry. For your sake."

"And hers." Clint picked up a cookie. "She doesn't need some Nosy Nellie digging into her past."

He devoured the cookie as Natalie pushed the kids on the swings. She hovered over them as they kicked a ball around the yard and dug in the small sandbox. Eventually, she returned to the table and sat down.

Lisa apologized. "I had no right to pry into your life or Clint's. Heaven knows, I would have broken an ankle running away if anyone had interrogated me when I first arrived here." She offered her hand. "Friends?"

After a long, slow, considering look, Natalie accepted the hand-shake. "Friends."

She was taking a risk, inviting another person into her circle, and she knew it. But in the three weeks she'd been in town, the only people she'd seen were the doctor, his nurse, Clint and the cashier at the grocery store. She'd never been a social butterfly, by any means, but she was tired of seeing the same few faces over and over again. Now that her feet were healed, she didn't even see the doctor anymore. Besides, Clint had already brought Lisa and Amy around, so they knew about her. With luck, Lisa's past and desire to keep her life secret would help keep her mouth shut.

Later, when she found the right way to word it, Natalie intended to find a way to ask Lisa to keep her presence in Haven a secret. The trick would be how to say it.

"So, you know I'm a widow. Amy is my life now. She keeps me busy. If you don't mind, I'd like to have Mathew over to play some-time. The company would be good for both of them. And for me."

Could Natalie allow that and still maintain her anonymity? "Um, I guess that would be okay." From the corner of her eye, she noticed Clint making a discreet cutting motion with his hand and glaring at Lisa.

"What?" Natalie pivoted and pinned Clint with a hard stare.

"Nothing."

"Don't give me that. Why are you glaring at her?"

Clint looked around the yard, refusing to meet Natalie's scrutiny.

"Dammit, Clint." Lisa turned to Natalie. "He told me he thought you were hiding from someone. And I was supposed to be your friend, no pressure, no games. No prying." She shrugged eloquently. "Apparently, inviting you to visit doesn't fit his protocol for low key."

"It doesn't. If she goes traipsing all over town, people are going to notice her. How could they not?" His fingers drummed restlessly on the table. "Haven is small—hell, it's tiny. Strange faces don't show up often, and people talk."

Natalie's gaze jumped between the two as they argued.

"People are talking already," Lisa informed him. "And it's not my doing." She gave Natalie an apologetic look. "Sorry. But the night you arrived, you interrupted a post rehearsal-dinner party for Grace and Sterling. Grace runs the bookstore. When you came in, Doc sent everyone home. The whole freaking town knows you guys are here. They know where you're living, and they're curious about who you are and why you aren't seen much."

Panic flooded through Natalie. Her palms started sweating, and her heart pounded. It was all she could do to sit still. She and Mathew had to go. If people were already talking, it wouldn't be long until Stanley showed up looking for her. She had to get rid of Clint and Lisa so she could pack. She'd grab Mathew and take the first bus out of town. "Oh, God, when is the next bus? Do buses even come here?"

"Buses?" Clint sounded confused.

"What about buses?" Natalie flushed. God, had she been talking out loud?

"Where do you think you're going?"

"I was thinking of moving on." *Don't panic. Get rid of them and pack.*

"I thought your car was smashed up? Oh, yah. That would explain the buses."

"You don't need to leave. You're safe here. Nobody will say anything about you." He placed his hand on top of hers.

Natalie jerked her hand away from Clint's soft touch and leapt to her feet. She paced circles around the table. "They're already talking." She scanned the yard, almost expecting to see people hiding behind one of the large trees. "You heard Lisa. People are gossiping already. I have to go. We have to go." She started toward the trailer.

Clint's hand on Natalie's shoulder stopped her in her tracks. "Relax, Natalie. You're safe here. Haven is a small town, but we protect our own."

"That's just it! I'm not one of Haven's own. I'm an outsider. People are talking." She jerked free of his touch.

Lisa rose slowly and stepped between Natalie and the trailer. "Relax, Nat. This is a small town. There isn't much going on. All newcomers are subject to a bit of gossip. But you live here now."

"So what? This situation is only temporary." She ignored the pained looked that crossed Clint's face.

"That doesn't matter. You live here now. We talk amongst ourselves, but not to strangers. We keep ourselves secluded. That's why we chose to settle here. Besides, if anyone sees you, and sees what's left of those bruises, they'll know why you're hiding. That'll keep their mouths shut for sure."

Natalie tried to step around Lisa, but Clint blocked her way, forcing her to remain on the deck. She twitched with irritation. Her fight or flight instinct kicked in big time.

"Come to the party on Saturday. It's already Thursday. Stay, let Mathew enjoy the party. Then on Sunday, when the weekly bus comes, you can leave if you still want to." Lisa took a small step backward, clearing the way to the door.

"There's only one bus a week?"

"Well, this is the back of beyond." Clint laughed. "You said so yourself. Frankly, for me, the slow pace and lack of strangers is a big part of Haven's charm."

"But what if Stan— But I want to go now." She groaned in distress, realizing she'd almost said her husband's name aloud.

"Look, if you need to leave, I'll drive you wherever you want to go. No strings, no questions. I'll just drive you and drop you off." His words were soft and conciliatory.

"Haven is small. You're safe here. I don't know why you're hiding. And I don't care. I want you to feel safe. Don't run away because of one party. Stay. Skip the party. Let those feet heal. Let Mathew play. I can bring Amy to visit. You can stay secluded here." She touched Natalie's hand. "I know what it's like to be scared. Don't let that panic overwhelm you."

"You have friends here." Clint gestured to himself and Lisa. "Lisa and I will look out for you."

Tears slid down Natalie's cheeks. "Why are you being so kind?"

Lisa shrugged and stepped in to hug Natalie. "I don't know about Clint, but when Davin and I got here, we were scared shit-less, running and hiding. It gets old real fast. But Haven felt safe for us. The people were kind. They rallied around to help us. For me, maybe it's a karma thing. Someone helped me; I want to help you."

Knowing Lisa had been through a similar situation eased a bit of the stress. Natalie looked from Lisa to Clint and then to the kids playing in the small sandbox across the yard. It had been a long time since Mathew had played with such abandon. Could she risk it? Could she stay in Haven for a while longer?

Slowly, carefully, she went over her actions since her abrupt departure from home. She hadn't used her debit or credit cards. She'd left her cell phone behind, and the car didn't have a GPS. She hadn't talked to anyone on the way, except at the gas station. Maybe it was okay to stay here for a while.

"Where is my car?"

"It isn't drivable."

"I know. Where is it?" she demanded with a pleading look.

"In that shed. Locked up." Clint waved toward a windowless building behind the garage. "The ragtop is shredded. I put it inside, hoping to dry it out. It got soaked in the downpour the night you crashed. I used my shop-vac to suck up as much water as I could, but you can't drive it. It has no wheels."

She smiled gratefully. "It's inside? Out of sight?"

Clint nodded.

Could she risk it? Could she take a chance and stay in this remote mountain town? The car she had "borrowed" was hidden. If she kept Mathew and herself secluded, they might be okay. Stanley wouldn't think to search for his pampered wife in the middle of nowhere. Would he? A tiny spark of hope ignited, the first positive outlook since that moment when Clint's flashlight had blinded her on her way up the slippery mountain slope.

"Okay, I'll stay." She released her breath slowly, praying she'd made the right decision.

Together, Clint and Lisa hugged her.

"You won't regret it." Lisa patted Natalie's shoulder. "And you don't have to come to the party."

More tears slipped down Natalie's face. She wasn't used to such kindness. Not from the people she knew and certainly not from strangers. But these tears were different. They tasted of relief, not sadness and fear.

"I'll think about the party." She gave a hiccupping laugh.

Slowly, Clint stepped back. "I hate to go, but I really should get back to the garage." He smiled at Natalie. "I'm glad you decided to stay. I'll pop back later for my laundry." He stepped off the deck and glanced over his shoulder. "See you at work tomorrow, Lisa."

Mathew and Amy raced to the fence and called their goodbyes, while Lisa and Natalie silently watched him go.

"He's a good man," Lisa observed once he was out of earshot.

"He's certainly been good to us." Was he too good to be true? After an unhappy childhood and a brutal marriage, Natalie was unaccustomed to kindness without strings. Few of her friends would do something without expecting a return favor. Except for Belinda. They hadn't kept in touch much over the years, just an occasional email or a letter, but Belinda had never asked for anything except friendship. It was difficult keeping in touch with her though, since Belinda's husband was sick and Nat depended on Clint for a phone. But it was time to make an effort. Natalie made a silent vow that, the next time she had access to a computer, she'd drop her old friend a line. Maybe, it was time to reconnect and make some friends, no strings attached. She could use more friends like Clint.

"Why is he like that?"

"Like what?" Lisa shook her head in confusion, her short blonde hair flittering around her face.

"He's been nothing but kind to us. It's like he can't do enough to help us." Natalie squinted her eyes against the late afternoon sun and stared at Clint's back.

"Oh, that." Lisa looked between Natalie and Clint several times, her gaze following him until he was out of sight. "He's a good guy."

"He helped Mathew and me up that hill, towed my car and stored it. He took us to the doctor, took us into his home, fed us and gave us a place to live. He hasn't asked for anything. What's the catch?"

"Why does there have to be a catch?"

"Come on, Lisa. There's always a catch. People don't just help other people. They always want something." Natalie knew she sounded hard and cynical.

"Do you think I came over today because I wanted something from you?"

The hurt in Lisa's voice surprised Natalie. "Didn't you?"

"I came because Clint is my friend and he thought you might need a friend." She crossed her arms and hugged herself. "I don't understand your cynicism. Can't people just be nice?"

"In my experience? No. They can't. There's always an ulterior motive." Her words were mocking, bordering on rude.

"Wow." Lisa shook her head. "I don't know where you came from, but it must have been an awful place. Davin and I ran away because my parents didn't want us together. But not for one minute did I wonder if they loved me. I always knew they wanted the best for me and my sisters. They thought Davin and I rushed into a relationship." She looked Natalie up and down, taking in her designer clothing and expensive rings. "You come from money, don't you?"

"I've never lacked for anything I needed. What difference does it make?" What was the point of the question?

"It makes me glad I grew up middle class then." She shrugged and turned to watch the kids playing. "If money makes you cold and selfish, I'm glad I had no part of it. Amy, don't climb the fence," she called to her daughter, who was rapidly scaling the gate. "Get down from there."

When Amy obeyed without complaint, she thanked her.

"I've never not had money," Natalie confessed. "And I've only known a few people who would offer help without questioning me. Clint is one of them."

Lisa turned and smiled at Natalie. "I do believe I've already agreed with that. Clinton Dawson is one of the good guys. He's done a lot of things for a lot of people here. And I cannot think of a single time he's asked for anything in return. Ask anyone in town."

"I thought you said this town protected its own?" Natalie's tone was critical. "Why would they tell me anything?"

"Because he's a good man." She huffed out a frustrated breath. "It's hard to explain. We gossip amongst ourselves, but we protect our own from outsiders. Maybe, it's a small-town thing. We help each other out." She smiled broadly. "Kind of like an old-time barn raising. Everyone kicks in."

"I'll take your word for it. But frankly, I don't get it." It was a concept so far removed from Natalie's experiences that she couldn't grasp it. Nor did she understand why Lisa was here.

"Come on, Natalie. Haven't you ever done someone a favor without asking for something in return? Ever?"

"I have…"

"See, it does happen. People chip in and help. Back home in the city, it was becoming a big deal. Random acts of kindness. Here, it's more a normal thing." Lisa sat at the table and patted the seat beside her. "Sit."

Without thinking, Natalie sat.

"Clint helps out because he wants to. I came over because I wanted to help him out. He mentioned you, and I thought you might need a friend, being all alone in a new place."

"Thank you. I appreciate it." Natalie's voice was quiet and grateful. "I was going a bit stir crazy without anyone to talk to."

Lisa laughed. "Hell, I know that. Spending the day with nobody but rug rats gets old. Fast. Welcome to Haven, Natalie. I hope we can be friends."

"Rug rats?" Natalie was unfamiliar with the term.

"Ankle biters, floor fleas. You know, kids?"

"Oh, I get it." She laughed. "Thank you for coming, Lisa. I'm still not sure why you did, but I appreciate it, and I could use a friend."

LATER THAT EVENING, Natalie settled into a chair to read, but she couldn't focus on the book. After reading the same sentences repeatedly, she gave up.

Was she like her friends? Cold and unfeeling? Self-centered? Vain and shallow?

Memories of her life passed by. She hadn't shared a real connection with anyone since Belinda. She circled through life with Stanley's rich friends but never really revealed anything about herself. In hindsight, she wasn't much better than they were. Sure, she gave the appropriate responses and did what was expected, but she hadn't really cared about them. With the exception of Mathew, she hadn't cared about anyone in a long time.

Shame filled her.

"Well, I won't be that woman anymore. I was no better than my father or Stanley. I'll find a way to make it up to the world."

CHAPTER 10

Natalie and Mathew stood hand-in-hand in front of the green house on Picket Drive, just down from Doc Hardy's house and clinic. She wasn't sure why she was here. She'd told Lisa they wouldn't come, but something drew her.

Children's laughter and kids' music flooded the street where Natalie stood, willing her heart to stop pounding and trying to find the courage to join the fun.

"Come on, Mommy. We go play? I hear kids." Mathew pulled her in the direction of the backyard.

Natalie looked at Mathew and smiled. His eager excitement was contagious. "Here, take this." She handed him a small, gaily wrapped package. "It's for Amy. It's her birthday." She hadn't told Mathew where they were going. She didn't want to disappoint him if she chickened out and couldn't bring herself to stop.

"Her biifday?" He hopped up and down. "Is there cake?" He bounced harder, joy lighting his face as he yanked on her arm.

"I don't know, sunshine. Let's go find out. When we get in the yard, say happy birthday and give her the present."

"Do I gets a present?" He balanced on his tiptoes, eagerly awaiting her response.

Kneeling down, her eyes level with his, she said quietly, "this is Amy's birthday. Today, she gets gifts." She ruffled his hair. "You'll get presents on your birthday. You get the fun of helping her celebrate her special day, and I think there will be cake for you."

"But I wanted a present."

"And you'll get a present on your birthday. But today is about Amy. She's your friend, and you like playing with her, right?" She waited for his reluctant nod before going on. "Today, we let her have the presents because we're glad she's our friend. Sometimes, we give things, instead of getting because it makes us happy to be nice to other people. Okay?"

Mathew sighed. "I guess."

It was obvious he didn't quite understand the concept of selfless giving. But was that really hard to believe? After all, until recently, it was a concept Natalie hadn't understood. Sure, she'd given gifts at the appropriate times, but she'd done so because it was the accepted protocol, not because she had any real interest in anyone else's happiness. Being in Haven and having friends who helped her without benefit to themselves had opened her eyes to the selfish life she'd lived as part of her privileged upbringing.

"You wait and see how happy she'll be when you give her that present. It'll make you feel nice, right here." She tapped him on the chest, over his heart. "Your heart will be glad."

"She's right." Clint's voice came from behind them.

"Oh, Clint, I didn't hear you." She turned to look at him and couldn't hold back her smile.

"I'm sneaky like that." He winked. "Mathew, I missed you. And, your mom is right. Doing nice things for people makes you feel good, too. It's an important part of being a friend."

"I don't have friends. Just mom and Colleen. She useded to look after me when Mom was busy."

"She was your nanny and your friend," Natalie reminded him.

"And now, you have lots of friends. Amy and her mom. There'll be other kids here, too, and soon, they'll be your friends. I think

Becky, Hayden, Win and Lee are coming. And I'm your friend, too."

"Yay, Mr. Clint is my friend," Mathew squealed and raced toward the gate, pulling Clint along with him. "Come on, Mommy."

She trailed slowly behind them, watching them together. In the short distance to the gate, Mathew managed to string together a number of questions, some rhetorical, some requiring answers. Words tumbled from him nonstop. Clint answered the way she would, with brief but complete answers.

"Come on, Nat. Are you having second thoughts?" Clint stopped, holding the gate open.

"What?" She'd stopped walking to watch the pleasant sight of Mathew interacting with a caring adult. "Oh, yes. I'm coming. I was just thinking."

"Just thinking about how great my butt looks in these jeans?" He waggled his backside in her direction.

"Well, no. But now that you mention it…" Her face warmed. She resisted the urge to fan the heat from her face. What the heck was she doing?

"Come on, woman. Let's do this." He wrapped his arm around her waist, dropped a quick kiss on her cheek and led her into the backyard.

The unexpected display of affection made her wobble on her feet.

Mathew waited at the corner of the house, twitching with impatience. "Come on. I wantsta play. They got a bouncy castle."

"They have a bounce castle," Natalie corrected him automatically.

"That's what I said." He gave her a look as if he wondered why she wasn't paying attention.

"Let's find Amy and give her the gift first. Then you can go play."

"She's over there, Sport." Clint pointed to the deck, where a cluster of people stood around the birthday girl.

"Sport? Mommy, Mr. Clint called me Sport again. Daddy never calls me anything 'cept Mathew." He looked sad and forlorn.

"Your father doesn't like pet names." Natalie banked down exasperation. Nothing slipped by this kid.

"Pet names?" He blinked up at her, momentarily distracted from the party. "Like doggy?"

"Pet names are special names that people use for each other. Like when I call you Sunshine or Matt."

"Or when I call you Sport."

"Oh." He grinned. "I like pet names." He raced toward Amy.

"Your husband doesn't have a pet name for him? I thought all parents had special names for their kids."

"My husband?"

"One can hardly miss that gigantic rock" He lifted her hand to examine her wedding rings. "Why didn't you call him after your accident?"

"Lots of people don't call their kids by short names. And I don't want to talk about my husband. That part of my life is over."

"Yet you still wear your rings?"

She knew the simple question implied a deeper layer of questions. Questions she wasn't prepared to answer. Instead, she walked away from him. It wasn't the first time in her life she'd rudely walked away from another person, completely ignoring their question. But it was the first time she was bothered by her rudeness.

She stopped and turned to look at him. "I'm sorry. That was uncalled for." She took a deep breath. Then she took another. "My past is full of ugliness. I prefer not to discuss it. I just want to stay here without history catching up to me. Please forgive me."

He studied her before nodding. "One more question. If I may?"

"Um. Okay. But I reserve the right to refuse to answer it." She grinned cheekily at him and wondered why she was so relaxed.

"Are you considering staying in Haven? For a while, at least?"

"That's two questions." She shook her finger at him. "I said one. But yes, I am considering staying. For a short time."

His smile lit his whole face and made the light in his eyes dance. "I'll take that answer! Come on." He grabbed her by the hand. "Let's go say hi to the birthday girl."

NATALIE STOOD BESIDE THE HOUSE, half tucked into a corner where she could keep her eye on Mathew. Every unfamiliar face seemed sinister and ominous. Any of these people could be one of Stanley's spies. A few people smiled in her direction. She smiled back, trying to find the balance between being friendly, and not inviting unwanted attention. After a while, she realized the guests were longtime locals, and her tension started to ease. She began to enjoy the party. She met dozens of new people, none of whom pried into her past. Most welcomed her to Haven and let her presence go at that. She soon found herself relaxing and people watching.

Havenites were different from her usual social circle. Cowboys mixed with stay-at-home moms. Doc Hardy and his nurse, Jessie, were there. Natalie met the banker, the mayor and their wives. Harmony Farnsworth, the lady she'd heard on the truck's radio the night she'd crashed, was a riot. She was full of life and laughter and spit out the most shocking comments.

Harmony walked up to Natalie, as bold as brass, and introduced herself. "So, you arrived with Clinton? Didn't ya? Well, I'll be. Good to see some sexy young thing snatch him up. He's one smokin' hot guy, our Clinton. 'Bout time someone put that manhood to good use!" She winked outrageously and laughed. "Why if I was ten years younger, I'd take him for a test-drive myself." She waggled her finger flirtatiously at him. "Yes, indeed. I'll bet he could ride ya 'til you couldn't walk straight."

Natalie nearly choked on her drink at the comments. "Gah," she, sprayed iced tea across the yard.

Harmony laughed. "Don't be fretting yourself, girlie. I may be old, but I ain't dead yet." She snickered, leaned on her cane and strolled away.

"Don't let her get your goat."

Natalie turned toward a soft, feminine voice.

A pretty woman about five six, with curly blonde hair and laughing eyes, stood arm-in-arm with a well-muscled, dark-haired man. "She says the damndest things just to get a rise out of people, but the woman's got a heart of gold."

"Hi." Natalie felt obligated to speak.

"I'm Grace. This is my husband, Sterling. You're Natalie?"

Natalie blinked in surprise. They knew her? Of course they knew her. Lisa had told Natalie how her unexpected arrival had interrupted a post-rehearsal dinner.

"Uh, yeah. I'm Natalie. Sorry about your party." How did one apologize for ruining a party?

Sterling laughed. "Thank God you arrived. I thought the party would go on forever."

Grace slapped playfully at his arm. "Doofus." She snuggled into his embrace. "He's just saying that because before the party he was gone for two weeks and wanted to be alone with me."

"You know it. I missed you like crazy." He pulled Grace into a tight embrace and kissed her long and slow. "I waited years for you."

Uncomfortable with their intimate kiss, Natalie didn't know where to look, so she glanced away. She'd never been kissed that way. Passion like that was the stuff of fantasy, of Hollywood, but it was easy to imagine being kissed like that. Wrapped tightly in a man's arms. In Clint's arms. Held close. His hands caressing her back, leaving fire in their wake. His lips both hard and soft caressing hers, demanding a response.

"I haven't seen you in my bookstore yet." Grace's words drew Natalie back into the conversation.

"I've been meaning to come by. I've already devoured the few novels Clint left in the trailer. I could use something new to read." Not that she had money to spare for books.

"It's a fabulous store." Sterling kissed the top of Grace's head. "She has the best collection of books. New, used, classics, kids' books, fiction, nonfiction. You name it. She has it. If she doesn't have it, she'll get it."

"Stop." Grace blushed and wrapped her arm around his waist.

Sterling laughed. "I'm her biggest fan."

"Books are my biggest weakness. I'll have to stop by and find myself a little escape." Lord knows, she could use the reprieve. She hated lies, even partial lies. She wanted to purchase a book, but she was barely able to afford food, and clothing for herself and Mathew. Beyond that, she had car repairs to consider. Books were a luxury she couldn't afford right now, but that didn't lessen her sincere desire to visit Grace's shop and check it out. For a moment, intense anger grew toward Stanley. He was living high on the hog without a care in the world, and she wasn't even scraping by. She would have to do something about that. The question was what?

"I'll stop by on Monday when Mathew and I go for our walk. If that's okay with you?" She didn't want to put Grace to any trouble.

"We're open ten until six Monday to Saturday." Grace laughed.

"And she's always there. Now, if you ladies will excuse me, I have a crisis to attend to." Sterling nodded toward a petite blonde girl crying hysterically outside the bouncy castle. "Miss Sasha seems to be having a meltdown."

"Sterling." Grace placed a restraining hand on his arm. "That's her temper tantrum cry. She isn't hurt."

He shrugged. "What can I say? I'm a helpless male against a female in distress. I shall distract the fair maiden lest she ruin the feast for the peasants." He bowed low to Grace, then to Natalie, the gesture both courtly and mocking. "My ladies, I bid you adieu."

Grace smiled at the back of her retreating husband. "That man has no restraint when it comes to Sasha. Four years old and she's still his master. But he's getting better." There was no censure in her voice, only fondness.

"I see Sasha is at it again." Clint strolled up to them, rolling his eyes.

"She is. It's the age, I'm afraid. Everyone talks about the terrible twos, but not once did anyone mention the fearsome fours or the agonizing almost five's."

"Yah, my sister mentioned that," Clint agreed.

"You have a sister?" Grace and Natalie chimed in unison.

"Well, I have two half-sisters and a half-brother." He shrugged dismissively and looked at the ground.

"I've known you for almost two years, and you've never mentioned a family." Grace poked him in the chest. "I thought we were friends."

"And we're not going to talk about them now. My father was a wastrel, and my siblings aren't much better. I choose not to have anything to do with them."

There was a cold, hard set to his shoulders, and his lips were pressed firmly together. He looked…angry.

"Well, if it's any consolation, my family isn't the greatest either," Grace admitted.

"Nor mine." Natalie scanned the yard, realizing she'd let her vigilance slip.

"Can't choose your relatives." Grace shrugged. "But you can choose your friends. And I'm hoping you'll choose to be mine, Natalie."

"Why? You don't even know me." Haven was the strangest place. Everyone wanted to be friends with everyone.

"Do I need a reason?" Grace countered.

"I suppose not." Natalie wrapped her arms around her waist.

"You sound skeptical." Grace smiled. "Let me tell you something. Three years ago when I arrived here, I couldn't believe how friendly the people were. Frankly, it was off-putting. It wasn't what I was used to. After a while, the kind-heartedness grows on you."

"O-kay…"

"Really, it does. Doesn't it, Clint?"

They turned to consider him.

"She's right, Natalie. There is something about this place. At the risk of sounding hokey, Haven is magical."

Natalie laughed outright at the absurdity of his statement. "Uh-huh."

"Seriously, look around you." He waved expansively, encompassing the entire oversized yard. "You've got a world of social classes all mingled together. The Joneses have almost no money." He waved at a smiling couple in well-worn but spotless clothes across the yard. Doc has money to burn. I'm comfortable."

"I was destitute when I arrived here." Grace picked up his theme. "Now, I live with Sterling in the big yellow monstrosity of a house on Third. And we're all here together. We get along. We help each other out."

"And no one fights?" Natalie's voice was laced with derision.

"Good gravy, no, we fight like cats and dogs," a new voice chimed in. Natalie turned toward the voice. A petite octogenarian hobbled toward her, leaning heavily on two canes.

"Natalie," Clint waved at the newcomer, "meet Gypsy Rose. Gypsy, Natalie."

"Hi." Natalie offered her hand awkwardly.

Gypsy leaned on one cane, handed the other to Clint and shook Natalie's hand. Her grip was strong and firm. "Nice to meet you. When you get used to Haven, you'll love it here. We fight. Sometimes, we have epic battles. But they never last."

"Gypsy's family settled here ages ago." Grace gave a wave toward Gypsy.

"Mid-eighteen-hundreds sometime." Gypsy smiled. "My family

was Romanian gypsy herbalists. Hence, my ridiculous name." She laughed lightly. "Got this far in the trek west and stalled. Story says our caravan got snowed in. Weather was different back then."

"They survived a whole winter in the mountains, alone? This place must be desolate in the winter." It was almost more than Natalie could fathom.

"Worse than desolate. It's freezing and lonely." Gypsy laughed again. "But not alone. They stumbled upon a trapper who took them in and helped them survive. My great-great-grandmother fell in love with that trapper and married him. Well, not all legal-like. But they stayed together. My family has been here ever since." She paused. "What was my point?"

"The fighting," Clint reminded her gently.

"Yup. We fight, but this place has special qualities. Folks who settle here stay here, and they get along. My old grandmother said something about ley lines or power lines or some such nonsense. When I was younger, I didn't believe her. I do now. This place is special. We named it Haven for a reason." She waggled her cane at Natalie.

Turning, Gypsy tapped Clint smartly on the shoulder with the handle of her cane. "And you, boy. Fetch me a beer."

"As my lady wishes." He offered his elbow and led Gypsy off in the direction of the coolers.

Natalie stared after them. "He isn't giving her a beer, is he?"

"Definitely not." Grace laughed. "Well, technically, yes. Near-beer. It's alcohol-free beer. It was Doc's idea, and since Gypsy can't see well enough to read anymore, she's fooled."

"Doesn't anyone tell her? Or give her a real beer by mistake?"

"The entire town is in on the secret. It's what we do. We take care of our own."

"That's…sweet but hard to believe." Natalie shook her head.

"You'll get used to the idea. Take you, for example."

"What about me?"

"I'm going to help you out."

"With…what?"

"Don't sound so hesitant. I'm going to lend you some books." Grace's laughter rang across the yard, and several heads turned in their direction before turning back to their own conversations.

"Books?"

"Steamy, smutty romances with larger than life heroes." She wiggled her eyebrows suggestively.

"I can't afford to buy anything right now. I have car repairs to pay for." Nat smiled apologetically.

"I gathered that. Clint says your car was almost totaled, and he's having trouble getting parts. You aren't working. I've seen you price checking at the grocery store and searching your wallet." When Natalie opened her mouth to object, Grace held up a hand, forestalling her words. "Don't worry about it. My store is as much a library as a bookstore. It didn't start out that way. Initially, it was a new-books-only store. Then I sold some of my own used books. Then it kind of snowballed. First, I bought some secondhand ones, then traded used for used. Now, you can pretty much borrow any of the used ones. I do take a deposit, but you get it back when you return the book."

"That's incredible. Why would you do that? Don't you want to make money?" Natalie slapped a hand over her mouth. "Sorry, that was rude."

"Surprisingly, I do make money. Not much, but enough. The lending started because I wanted to share my love of reading with those less fortunate, like the Joneses. They didn't have any money for books for their sons, so I lent them a few. Haven's too small for a library, so I became the library. I only lend the used books, and I keep a decent stock of new ones. I can order in anything you want…if you don't mind waiting a week."

"Summer tourist business pretty much keeps her afloat all year." Sterling strolled up, carrying Sasha piggyback.

"Tourism? Haven hardly seems like a tourist hot spot." A frisson of unease skittered down Natalie's spine. "I mean, it's nothing but mountains, rocks and trees." Good thing she'd learned this was a tourist town before she became too comfortable. She'd have to stay sharp and keep her eyes open for strangers.

"There are two small lakes nearby and several small campgrounds. Summer means a lot of visitors and they're good for business. For all the businesses." Sterling slid Sasha from his back, into his arms. "Now, kiss your mom before we go home."

Sasha made kissy sounds toward Grace, with a pout on her face. "I don't want to go home. I wanna play in the bouncy."

"You, my darling, need a nap. The castle will still be here later. Go with Daddy. He needs a rest." Grace winked at her husband of only a few weeks. "Love you both to bits." She smiled and waved them off.

"He seems good with your daughter." Natalie's compliment was sincere.

"His daughter. Sasha is the daughter of my heart, not my biological daughter. I've known Sterl for years, but we've only just reconnected." She sighed and smiled sappily. "I did miss him."

"You look…lovestruck." Natalie envied their happiness.

Grace chuckled. "Indeed, I am. That man is the best thing that ever happened to me." She looped her arm through Natalie's. "Come on, my friend. With Sterl gone, you've just acquired a job as my barbeque assistant. We need to feed the ravaging horde."

"Isn't feeding the guests Lisa's job? It's her party." Shoot, she had to learn not to stick her nose in where it didn't belong. How Lisa chose to run the party was none of Natalie's business.

"Technically, yes. But I offered to pitch in so she could visit and supervise the kids. She baked my wedding cake, you know. The girl's got mad skills in the kitchen."

A hand brushed across Natalie's shoulder. Lisa stood behind her. The touch startled her, but it was too gentle to be one of Stanley's goons.

"Don't listen to her." Lisa laughed. "I can't cook worth beans. My dad once told me I should never cook again. But baking, that's easy as pie."

The trio laughed at the bad pun.

"I'm better than I used to be—necessity being the mother of invention, or in this case cooking. With Davin gone, I've had to adapt."

"Is Mathew allergic to anything? I'm breaking out the sunscreen and reapplying the lotion on all the kids before someone gets burned." Lisa scooped a tube of sunscreen off the table and gestured toward the yard with it.

"Good idea. His is probably worn off by now, and he doesn't have any allergies. I appreciate the thought, though."

"Not nearly as much as I appreciate not having to cook. *Ciao*, babies." She waggled her fingers and skipped off toward the castle.

Grace and Natalie chatted quietly, flipping burgers and roasting wieners. Several nearby tables were laden with salads and desserts. Three coolers of soda and beer packed in ice rested in the shade of the tables.

"Isn't this a bit overboard for a four-year-old's birthday?" Natalie took a small sip of white wine.

"A bit. But the town gathers a lot in the summer. Winter get-togethers are smaller and more subdued."

"Because it is as cold as…well, winter," Clint chipped in, stepping onto the patio, a platter of burger buns in his hand.

"Eloquent as always," Grace teased him.

"Winter gatherings are smaller and more intimate." He ignored the jibe. "We get together and snuggle under blankets and use our body heat to keep warm." He shoulder bumped Natalie.

Her mouth opened, closed, then opened again. "Um…"

"He's teasing. We do nothing of the sort. Though what happens in the privacy of your trailer is up to you…"

"I'll keep that in mind." They were both teasing her. "Maybe, I need to start looking closer at the menfolk."

Clint sputtered something unintelligible, and the women laughed and high-fived each other.

"Well played," Grace laughed.

"Maybe, that guy over there." Natalie gestured across the yard toward a tall, dark-haired, well-muscled, solid-looking man in his early thirties. "Who is that tall drink of water?"

"That's Mac. RCMP officer. Respectable, single, attractive. Kind of a catch, really."

"Oh, he is kind of cute."

Clint's shoulders tightened. His knuckles were white, and it looked as if he might snap the platter in half.

"He's not available." Clint stalked away from them.

"Actually," Grace whispered. "He is available. He's Clint's best friend. They've been hanging out together as long as I've been around. Not that you're actually interested." She shoulder bumped Natalie and laughed.

Dusk fell quickly, as it did in the mountains. Natalie had no idea where the day had gone. She was so wrapped up in meeting people and watching her son blossom under the praise and attention of their new friends. He was fast becoming gregarious, carefree and happy. Maybe, Haven was magic.

She smiled at her son where he sat, knee deep in the sandbox, playing with graders and loaders. "Come on, Mathew. Time to go home."

"I wanna play, Mommy. I likes it here." He wiggled farther away from her.

"We can come back another day. Look, even Amy is going inside now, and it's her birthday. Bedtime was an hour ago." She reached down and scooped him into her arms. That he let her pick him up without protest was a testament to how exhausted he was. She'd already said goodbye to Lisa, so Natalie headed for the gate and the short walk home. Stepping off the grass onto the sidewalk made her realize how exhausted she was. It was a wonder Mathew was functional at all. And her feet hurt. She'd thought them mostly healed, but perhaps, the long afternoon had been more than she'd anticipated.

"Do you want me to get my car? It'll only take a minute." Clint's voice came from behind her.

"No, thanks. It's only a couple blocks. I'll mange."

"Let me take him. You're mincing along. Your feet must be killing you."

She looked at Mathew, who had gone limp in her arms. Asleep. "Well, no bath for him tonight." She handed Mathew into Clinton's outstretched arms. "The kid weighs a ton when he's asleep. It's like trying to carry a forty-pound wet noodle."

Clint hoisted Mathew close and held him in a secure, gentle grasp.

"You make that look so easy. Thank you. My feet do hurt a bit."

"You should have taken it easy." He gave her a stern look.

"The day just blitzed by. I didn't even realize the time or that my feet hurt." She laughed self-deprecatingly as they walked. "Thank you for introducing me to Lisa. We get along well."

"You needed her." He shifted Mathew in his arms.

For a moment, Natalie bristled. She didn't need anyone. Did she? The only person she needed was Mathew. They didn't require anyone else. Did they?

They strolled quietly for a few minutes, their pace slow, Natalie walking on the lawn to cushion her feet. She had really enjoyed the day. She had a lot in common with Lisa, Jessie, Grace and everyone else at the party. They were a companionable group.

"You know what? I think I did need her."

"Does that shock you?"

"Not exactly. I'm not used to having close friends. Acquaintances, yes. Friends…not so much." She couldn't find quite the right words to explain her emotions. She settled on a vague hand gesture.

"I hope you consider me a friend, too." He pivoted to give her an outrageous wink.

She stopped and looked at him. "You know what? I do consider you a friend. You've been good to me. To us." She hadn't expected to find friends while on the run.

"Just a friend? I was hoping for more." His voice was teasing but carried a bit of…something more.

"Sorry, Clint. I'm not considering more than friendship. Hell, I wasn't even looking for that." Fear swamped her, and she lashed out. "Now, I'm stuck in this backwater town. I've got no car, no money. I can't get away. I'm stuck between the proverbial rock and a hard place with nowhere to run and nowhere to hide. The last thing I need is more." She stomped off.

Half a block later, she halted.

Mathew.

How could she have forgotten her son?

Sheepishly, she waited for Clint to catch up. When he came alongside, she resumed walking. She didn't say anything. How could she? She didn't have words for what she felt and was too afraid to share her fear of Stanley catching them.

Clint carried Mathew into the trailer and laid him gently on the bed. Quickly, Natalie washed her son's face and hands before slipping him into his pajamas. She ignored Clint watching her.

CLINT LEANED against the doorjamb while Natalie prepared Mathew for bed. The tenderness of her actions were not lost on him, nor did they come as a surprise. For a moment, he was jealous of her obvious affection for her son.

Her face shone with maternal love that warmed his heart. It reminded him of the times his mother had tucked him into his bed. Of her passion for life and the love she'd bestowed on him. There was something special about the bond between a boy and his mother.

Natalie was beautiful, and she was a good mother. Her smile lit up a room, and it lit up his heart. There was something about her that drew him, like a moth to a flame.

He felt good when he was around her. He thought about her often and found himself searching for excuses to be with her. Two days ago, he'd "accidentally" ripped his favorite shorts so he could ask her to mend them.

He just wished he knew what she was running from. Sure, he had his hunches. Only an idiot would be blind to the bruises she'd carried when she'd arrived in Haven. Not all of them had come from the accident. A fact clearly evident in the wariness she displayed around men. Once she got to know a man, the cautiousness eased. At least, it did around everyone but Clint. She held herself apart from him, and that frustrated the hell out of him.

He wanted, needed to hear the truth of her past, but he wanted to hear it from her. Every time the subject of her husband came up, it was as if a door slammed shut, locking Clint outside. Except for the massive diamond ring, she acted as if she didn't have a husband. Why didn't she want to talk about him? Who was he? And why was she running scared from him?

Day by day, she was becoming increasingly important to Clint, but the frustration of waiting for her to see him as more than a friend was aggravating.

Before long, he'd actually have to order the parts for her car instead of pretending he couldn't find them. She wasn't stupid; she'd catch on to the fact he was stringing her along to keep her in town. And he didn't think she'd buy the idea he just wanted to keep her safe. Once she realized he was stalling, it wouldn't take much of a leap for her to realize he wanted her for himself. Unless she warmed up to him, that could mean big trouble.

There had to be a way to find out who she'd been with before she'd arrived in Haven. He didn't want to irritate her or make her distrust him even further.

~

"YOU'VE GOT to be fucking kidding me." Lisa stared at Clint as if he'd grown three heads. "Seriously? You are the epitome of hypocrisy. You are certifiable." With each word, she stabbed Clint in the chest with her finger. "First, you tell me to be her friend without pushing her about her past. Then you want me to spy on her?"

Clint opened his mouth to explain.

"Don't say another word! I won't do it. No way! No how! Not ever." She stood staring at him, hands on her hips, and for a moment, he wondered if she'd start breathing fire.

"Of all the unmitigated gall, the conceit, the stupidity. Jesus. Clinton James Dawson, you're an idiot." She pivoted on her heel, stomped from his office and slammed the door.

"I'm still your boss," he called after her.

The door flew open and crashed against the wall. "The boss card? You're playing the boss card?"

Clint flopped into his desk chair and sighed. "No." Defeat washed over him. What the hell did he do now?

"Good!" She glared at him. "I like her, and I won't spy on her. Not even for you." She shook her head. "Why the urgent need to know about her past?"

"Someone hurt her, and I want to fix it." He shrugged, not knowing how to properly express his feelings.

"You can't. That's not how marital abuse works. She has to work her way past it. You can't save someone who refuses to stand up to their abuser."

"Can you at least find out her real name?" he pleaded.

"N. O. If you want to know her secrets, ask her. Do your own damn spying. Figure it out for yourself," she tsked loudly. "Men!"

"How do I find out information someone doesn't want to share with me?"

"Good grief. Google it. Ask her. Why are men so freaking stupid?" She covered her face with her hand and shook her head in exasperation. "And who the hell says it's any of your business anyway? Get a grip, Dawson. Leave her alone." She turned on her heel, pulled the door shut behind her and left him alone with his thoughts.

"Well, at least, she didn't slam it this time."

CHAPTER 11

Stanley wondered why he'd agreed to take Alisha to the club. Dinner was turning into a tedious affair.

His day had started like shit, with his investigator stating that after a month, he'd been unable to find any signs of Natalie. She hadn't used her debit card or any of her credit cards. The bitch had left her cell phone at home, and the car she'd taken didn't have a tracking device.

Her underhanded escape left him no choice but to report her as missing to the police and accuse her of kidnapping his son. The subsequent publicity debacle had been a nightmare. It wasn't often the wife of a high-profile, wealthy businessman ran away and abducted his child. It was taxing to play the grieving father and inconsolable husband, when all he wanted to do was find the bitch and beat the hell out of her.

Then, while he had his guard down, a competitor took advantage of his distraction, beat him to the punch and closed a long-term production deal with a small company Stanley had been trying to take over.

Now, he stared across the table at Alisha, wishing he'd just taken her home and fucked her. Didn't she know how annoying she was?

God, he was sick to death of women and their infernal games and endless needs. It was too bad she had such phenomenal talents in bed. For the first few years of their relationship, she'd been easy to control with money and gifts. Now, it was increasingly obvious she wanted more; she wanted a permanent place in his life and his home.

There was no way in hell that would ever happen. She'd come to the end of her usefulness. It was time to find another mistress. He'd pay off Alisha, and she'd be out of his life.

She sat across from him, sleepy-eyed, her hair styled to look sexy and tousled. Her tongue darted out to lick her parted lips. Her foot slid up the inside of his leg, her fingertips trailing the edge of her plunging neckline.

Instantly, he was rock hard.

Okay, he wouldn't break it off tonight. He had to have her one more time.

"Come on, Alisha. Time to go." He shoved his chair back and jerked to his feet.

"But I haven't had dessert yet." She pouted.

"I'll give you dessert." He formed the sentence as a sexual invitation. "Let's go." He knew she'd object again, so he offered the one stimulus he knew she wouldn't be able to resist. "Let's go to my house for an after-dinner drink."

"You're going to let me see your home?" She seemed surprised. Her eyes flashed with excitement, and she hurried to her feet.

"Put it on my tab." Stanley handed the waiter a generous tip, then with his hand on the small of Alisha's back, rushed her out the door.

~

"You make love like a god." Alisha planted small kisses along his shoulder.

Stanley snorted dismissively but didn't spare her a glance. "You better head home. I'll call you a cab." He'd taken her roughly, just the way he liked it.

"Your home is wonderful." Alisha attempted to prolong her visit. Her arms wrapped around his waist, and she rubbed sinuously against him. "I want to make love with you in front of that fireplace." She waved toward a towering marble fireplace with a plush oriental rug before it.

"Not tonight." He pulled out his cell phone and ordered a taxi for her. He was done with her now. A quick tour of his house had been followed by an even quicker interlude in the sitting room.

That would show the bitch. He'd fucked Alisha on the bed he'd shared with his wife. It was a degrading shot at both women, and even though Natalie wasn't there to discover his wrongdoing, it gave him a sense of superiority to disrespect her so blatantly. He'd have to tell her about it when she finally hauled her ass home.

"Anything you wish, darling." She kissed him on the cheek and fondled his hand.

Stanley stared at her. She had a glint in her eye that disturbed him.

"Listen." He eased her back a step. "We're done."

"Done?" Her face paled. Her full attention snapped to him.

"Done. Finished. Kaput." He pulled a wad of cash from his pocket and handed it to her. "Your rent is paid for the rest of this month. Be out by the thirty-first. This relationship is over. I'll notify the landlord you're leaving. I'll send your severance check in the mail. No need to come to the office. You've been replaced." He didn't even flinch at the lie. He hadn't replaced her. Yet! But he would. Receptionists were a dime a dozen to a man like him.

He waved at the front door. "Go. It's over. We're over."

"Over?" Tears welled in her eyes. "How can it be over? I love you."

"Alisha, don't be so stupid. You were my mistress, my fuck buddy. Your time in my life is over." His voice dripped disdain. He stepped toward her menacingly, using his body to propel her toward the front door.

"It can't be over! Why'd you even bring me here?" Her voice was frantic. She tried to kiss him, to draw him back to her.

"Get out." He shoved her away.

"I'll do better next time. Please don't send me away." She quivered when he raised his hand. "Please."

He slapped her hard, knocking her back a step. "I said we're done."

"Please, Stanley, don't send me away. I'll do anything you want." Desperation dripped from her words.

It sickened him.

He drew back his fist and slammed it into her gut. Once, twice, then a third time. She buckled under the assault and dropped to her knees.

"What did I do?" She tried to roll over when she finally regained the breath he'd knocked out of her.

"You're clingy, and I'm tired of you."

"I don't need to live with you," she moaned, referring to their earlier discussion of replacing his wife. "I'm content with our arrangement. I won't ask for anything more."

"Shut the fuck up." A vein popped and jumped in his neck. "Get out." He waved a fist at her cowering form and delivered a well-aimed kick to her thigh.

Tears rolled down her cheeks, unchecked. She huddled against the floor, whimpering.

"Stop your damned whining and leave."

Slowly, she inched to her knees, her eyes never leaving his face. "Please, just give me one more chance."

He stepped around her, yanked her to her feet and pushed her through the door. "Goodbye, Alisha." He slammed the door behind her. "Don't bother calling or texting me."

CHAPTER 12

The Book Nook comprised the entire first floor of what had once been an eight-room, Victorian-styled house. The walls had been removed to reveal one big room with support pillars holding up the second floor. Situated on Main Street, the house had large windows and a deck that wrapped nearly the entire way around. Inside, there was a small storage area, a kitchen, a staff room, a children's play area and plenty of retail space. It smelled like cookies, coffee and books. To Natalie, it smelled like heaven.

From where they sat in the coffee shop area of Grace's bookshop, Natalie and Grace watched Mathew and Sasha playing in the well-equipped playroom.

"I can't believe how you've got the kids' area set up. Toys, games, video games, a reading area, building blocks and a ball pit. It must have cost you a fortune." It felt strange to think about money. It had never been a concern before. Now, she seemed obsessed with it.

"Actually, a lot of the toys were donated by people whose children had outgrown them. The rest I consider money well spent. The toys serve two purposes really. They keep the kids entertained and out of their parents' hair, giving them more time to browse or relax. That turns into money in my pocket."

"So it's kind of a win-win situation." Natalie sipped her coffee. "It's sure working for me. It's nice to get out of my own yard for a bit."

"And nice for me, too. Sasha is going stir crazy in here alone. She really misses her daycare. She loves the other kids."

"I heard Emily is away," Natalie sympathized.

"Yeah. Her sister had a baby by emergency C-section, so Em is helping out for a bit, which leaves me without childcare."

"Why didn't you ask me to help?" It was so typically Haven to pitch in, that Natalie was a bit surprised Grace hadn't asked.

"She'll be back on Monday. Sterl will be home from the city tonight. So, I've got it covered."

"You know I would have helped you out, right?"

"Honestly, I didn't think of you. You've only been in town for a couple months. I rarely have the chance to see you, and I didn't want to impose." Grace blushed. "I promise to ask next time, but you have to promise to ask if you need help." She gave Natalie a telling look.

"I promise," Natalie vowed, wondering if Grace knew her real reason for stopping by the bookstore. Since there was no point in guessing, she looked around the store, and seeing only Harmony, the local gossip, she whispered a confession. "Grace, I'm going to be frank. I have a problem."

"Is there anything I can do to help?"

"Well, there might be." Natalie struggled for words. It wasn't easy asking for help. Before she'd left Stanley, she hadn't needed help. And when the abuse had become too much and threatened to spill over to Mathew, there had been no one to turn to. Now, Grace waited patiently for her answer, and she couldn't form the words to ask.

"Excuse me for a minute." Grace set down her cookie on her

plate. "I just need to check if Harmony needs anything. Keep an eye on Sasha for me. I won't be long."

"Harmony," Grace walked over to the elderly woman, "is there anything I can help you find today? We've got a couple new Regency romances I think you'll enjoy."

"Oh, good." Harmony's voice betrayed her disappointment at having her eavesdropping interrupted.

"Let's just get you set up." Grace pulled a couple books off the shelf and led the older woman to a chair in the opposite corner of the store near the front windows. "Sit here, in the sun, and check these out. I know you're going to love them."

Harmony hmphed and sat down with the books.

"Give me a shout when you've decided. I'll just be in the back with Natalie." She walked back to the coffee area and winked at Natalie as she sat. "Now, you don't have to worry about being overheard. What can I do for you?"

"Well…" Natalie blushed. "This isn't easy for me. Before I came to Haven, I never had to worry about anything. Or ask anyone for help." She sighed and rubbed her forehead. Finally, she worked up the courage to spit it out. "I heard you're looking for summer help. I want the job."

"You know it's minimum wage, right?"

"I assumed so. But, frankly, I need the money to survive. We need groceries. My savings are almost gone. You need help. I need a job. I thought maybe we could help each other out." Natalie hated the pleading tone that crept into her voice.

"Have you ever worked retail?" Her tone was nonjudgmental.

"Honestly, no. But I'm an avid reader and I learn fast." This was so awkward.

"Okay. Trial basis to start. That's standard for everyone I hire. What I've learned is not everyone is cut out for retail. It takes patience."

"Thank you so much." Natalie jumped to her feet and hugged her friend.

"Wow," Grace laughed. "I didn't expect that kind of gratitude."

"You have no idea how much this means to me or how badly I need this job." Natalie sat and took a gulp of her coffee.

"I think I do. I told you before, I've seen the way you double check every price when you shop and how rarely you splurge on anything, even on a coffee for yourself."

Natalie ducked her head to hide her shame.

"Don't. Don't do that."

"Do what?"

"Don't be ashamed of needing money. It happens to everyone."

"Not me." Natalie hated the heat that rose in her cheeks.

"No?" Grace said with a bit of teasing in her voice. She waved at Natalie's clothing. "High-end labels like you wear? Those don't come cheap. I know that personally. It took me a long time to adjust to not having money." She paused to wave at her employee as she came through the door and ducked behind the counter to start her shift.

"You?" Natalie faltered, not knowing how to express her question.

"Me." Grace laughed.

"But you're so…casual." Natalie floundered. "That is…I mean…oh, God. I've stuck my foot in my mouth again." She closed her eyes and sighed.

"I know exactly what you mean. Frankly, I came from money. My family ruled my life with zero room for self-exploration or deviation from the plan they set out for me. The best schools, the best college and the degree they chose. I got sick of it and ran away from home. Twenty-two years old and I ran away from home. It was the smartest thing I ever did."

"You ran away? At twenty-two?" Natalie couldn't believe what she was hearing.

"I took the first bus out of Calgary. I only had enough money to get to Drayton Valley. It wasn't far, but Drayton wasn't the sort of place my family would look for me. Eventually, after a lot of job hopping, I ended up in Haven. I didn't plan anything. I just got fed up and ran, leaving my cell phone and credit cards behind. All I knew was I had to prove I could make it alone. And I darn near starved to death before I found a job. Thank God I managed to scrounge a job at this bookstore." She looked fondly around the store she now owned. "Frankly, I think Mavis hired me because she felt sorry for me. Lord knows, her heart wasn't into running the place." She paused and looked at Natalie. She sipped her coffee. "So, I know what you're feeling. I recognize the terror and elation of making it on your own. I don't know your story, but I do know it was ugly, even if it was privileged. That's why I'm going to hire you. A chance to start again, to make it on your own. Paying it forward." She shrugged off the importance of the job. "It isn't much. Minimum wage and all the coffee you can drink."

"I'll take it." Natalie breathed a grateful sigh.

"I think Emily has a space open in her daycare. You can ask her when she gets back next week. A couple of the local girls can babysit evenings."

"Evenings?"

"I'm open longer hours during the summer. You'll need to be available two evenings a week."

"Oh. I hadn't thought of that. I don't like leaving Mathew…" She trailed off.

"It'll be okay. This is a small town. You'll only be five minutes from home, even on foot. If something happens, you're only seconds away."

"I suppose." She thought about it for a few minutes. "Okay. I guess it will do Mathew good to be away from me a bit." She didn't sound convincing, but at least she sounded willing.

"Besides, I'm sure Clint will babysit." Grace nudged Natalie's foot with her toe.

"Uh-um. Why would he do that?" Natalie looked everywhere, except at Grace.

"Because, I adore your son." Clint startled both women.

"Geez. Stop sneaking up on me."

"He does that." Grace smiled at Clint. "He's the sneakiest man I've ever met. You turn around, and *boom!* There he is. It's rather disconcerting."

Clint grinned, turned a chair around and straddled it. "Any coffee for me?" He winked at Grace.

"You know where the pot is. I've never known you not to help yourself." Even as she said it, she stood. "I'll get you a cup just this once. But only because I have to get back to work." She looked at Natalie. "Get back to me after you talk to Emily. We'll work something out."

"Thanks. I appreciate it, more than you know." Natalie ducked her head.

"Pay it forward, my friend. Pay it forward." Grace gave a little finger wave and walked off.

"How can I ever repay her? Or you? Or half the town? Everyone's been so good to me." She looked at Clint, expecting him to provide the answer.

"Don't look at me." He flashed a warm smile. "Unless you want to have dinner with me?" His tone was nonchalant.

Natalie's heart pounded when she realized it was more than a casual request. What did he want from her? Hadn't she made it clear she wasn't interested in a relationship with him? No, that was wrong. She couldn't risk a relationship with him. With anybody. How did she say no without sounding like a witch? She'd grown used to having him in her life. She enjoyed being with him, and she liked the way Mathew had bonded with Clint; even though she knew it'd be hard on Mathew when she scraped up enough money to pay for her car and leave Haven. Strangely, the thought of leaving this town and its people hurt.

CHAPTER 13

Clint studied the sad expression on Natalie's face. "Why does sharing a meal with me distress you so much?"

"No. I was just thinking about moving on. I'll miss Haven."

"And will you miss me?" He tried teasing to lighten her unease.

She looked him up and down. Then she winked. "Yes. Yes, I'll miss you."

Surprise at her wink made him grin.

"After all, without your laundry and mending, I'll have hours of free time."

Clint laughed. It wasn't like Natalie to tease.

He liked it, and he liked the easy smile on her face. When she let her guard down, she was beautiful and almost more attractive than he could resist. His fingers tightened on the back of the chair until his knuckles went white. It was the only way he could keep from cupping her face in his hands and kissing those delectable pink lips.

"What? You look like you're going to snap that chair in half." She sounded concerned. "Are you okay?"

"No, I'm not okay. Frankly, I want to kiss you until neither of us can see straight."

"Oh."

He liked the breathless sound of her voice.

"Yes, I'll have dinner with you."

He smiled from ear to ear. "Good. I'll pick you up at eight."

"Eight?" she squeaked. "Mathew will be asleep."

"Exactly."

"But, I can't leave him alone. Can we go earlier?" She jumped up and paced.

"Eight. I'll bring a sitter. I want to be alone with you." He didn't give her a chance to respond. He just smiled enigmatically and walked away.

"MOMMY, WHERE DID MR. CLINT GO?" Mathew asked from the play area. "I want to play with him."

She smiled. "I don't know, Mathew. Back to work, I guess. We'll see him another day.

"But…" A full-blown temper tantrum was on its way.

She almost smiled again. Strangely, it delighted her to know her son was growing independent and developing his own personality. As much as she disliked his rare tantrums, they were a positive sign of a strong person to come.

"How about we see if Miss Grace will let us take Sasha to the park?" She cut his tantrum short.

"Yay," Mathew and Sasha squealed in unison.

"And Amy?" Mathew asked hopefully.

"We'll stop and ask Miss Lisa on the way."

Ten minutes later, everyone was slathered in sunscreen, Natalie had a backpack full of snacks, toys and drinks, and they were on their way.

NATALIE CHECKED to be sure Mathew was asleep before settling herself on the deck to wait for Clint. The evening was warm with just enough breeze to keep the mosquitoes off. By the time they were finished dinner, she'd need the sweater that sat beside her purse.

Dinner.

For the life of her, she couldn't figure out why she was having dinner with Clint. She rubbed her hands up and down her arms, trying to dispel her unease. Why had she agreed to go out with him?

"Why? Oh, God. Why did I agree?" She rose and paced the deck.

"Why? Because he's handsome. And kind. And good with Mathew." Her pacing quickened. "I don't need a man. I don't want a man." She tried to ignore the part of her heart that told her she *did* want a man. She just didn't want the one she'd been forced to marry.

Clint wasn't anything like Stanley. Not once had he lost his temper with her or Mathew. He didn't drink to excess, or rather, she'd never seen him drunk. The entire town liked and respected him. So, why did he make her so nervous?

The snick of the gate latch made her whirl around in surprise.

"Oh, you're here." She hated the way she sounded breathless. "Hi, Lisa," she added, belatedly noticing her friend was with Clint. "Where's Amy?"

"Amy is having a sleepover with Sasha," Clint said, smiling gratefully at Lisa.

"Clint figured I was the best man for the job, so I pawned my kid off on Grace."

"You didn't have to do that. We could have gone out another night." She half wished their date would be canceled.

"What? No way am I giving you a chance to back out on me. So, I begged Lisa and Grace to help me out."

"You shouldn't have done that." She felt rattled. Half angry, half thrilled.

"He should have, and he did. You haven't had a night out since you arrived. We knew you wouldn't feel right about using a local girl until you've had a chance to interrogate her yourself." Lisa walked past Clint and headed for the door. "Now, go." She made shooing motions with her hands. "Be off. Stay late. Let loose. Enjoy your evening. I have a date with a red-hot vampire." She waved a paperback novel as if cooling her face and faked a swoon. "Tootles." She slipped into the trailer.

Natalie watched her go inside, banking the sudden panic rising in her throat. She swallowed hard and forced her heart to stop racing.

"You look lovely tonight. I'm very glad you agreed to go out with me." The soft smile on his face added credence to his words. He offered her his arm. "Shall we?"

Natalie hesitated, took one step forward and then stopped. She chewed her lip nervously. "Just friends. Right?"

For a moment, he looked disappointed. "Just friends." He offered his arm again.

"Clinton…"

"As you wish. Friends. For now."

She gathered her things and took his arm. "So, where to?"

"Where are we going?" he asked in surprise. "Well, not the café in the garage. Not the bookstore or Rowdy's Bar. And since it's over an hour, one way, to the nearest town, that leaves only Sid's Steakhouse. Unless, you're willing to head out of town?" He left the suggestion hanging.

"I'm sure Sid's will be lovely." She pulled the gate closed behind them. "Though, I don't eat much red meat."

"Red meat is the only food." Clint bunched up his biceps and growled with a tough, he-man voice.

"Red meat goes straight to my hips." Natalie cast a rueful look at her curves.

"Red meat it is." Clint leered. "I adore your lovely curves."

"Oh, get real." She mock slapped his arm. "Men like stick-figure model types." They slowly walked down the tree-shaded sidewalk.

"Actually, men like curves."

"Bullsh—crap. I can't remember how many times Stanley told me real women didn't eat like pigs. They dined on salad and vegetables to stay thin and feminine." *Shit. Why did I have to say his name? Lord, don't let Clint notice.* Panic washed over her. She twitched nervously and tried not to hurry away.

STANLEY? Why did that name ring a bell? He mentally paired Natalie's last name and her husband's first name. Stanley Schwartz. Unease shifted over him. Something didn't feel right. He shook off the feeling.

"Assuming Stanley is your husband's name…let me be the first to tell you Stanley is an idiot. Men like curves. I," he put heavy emphasis on the pronoun, "adore curves." He smiled at her. "I much prefer being cuddled up to luxurious curves to hugging a bone-rack."

"Luxurious? What am I? A sports car?"

"Babe, if you were a sports car, I'd ride you until I ran out of gas."

Natalie glared at him, and his face flamed hot.

"Um. That's to say that I, er, um, you look lovely."

"I cannot believe you said that. You are such a chauvinist."

"Okay, I admit I can be a bit of a…a man, sometimes." He shrugged. "What can I say? I am a man, and I appreciate a shapely woman. Curvy, skinny, chubby… The wrapping really doesn't matter. It's what's inside that counts."

SHE SLOWED TO STUDY HIM. "You're serious?"

"Dead serious. I've dated a few women. Some were stunning, some were quite ordinary. But each of them were unique and had their own special charm."

"So, you get around then?" She squinted at him. He hadn't struck her as a player. But realistically, she hadn't dated much before marrying an awful man, so who was she to judge?

"At one time, I did, yes. But it's been years since a woman interested me enough that I asked her out. Hell, I'm practically a monk!"

"A monk? You?" Natalie laughed outright. "A monkey maybe."

"You mock me?" He clowned around, pretending to be an ape. "Seriously, Natalie. My last date was eight months ago when I took Harmony to the Harvest Ball."

"Harmony Farnsworth?"

"Harmony Farnsworth. Before her, it was the school teacher, and before that, the post-mistress. I haven't been on a date with someone under fifty since, well… it's been too long to remember." He stopped talking and chucked her under the chin. "You, Natalie Schwartz, are my first date in over three years." He touched her cheek softly. "From the moment my flashlight landed on you standing there, soaking wet in that gully, I've wanted you. You were so brave, so terrified, but so strong for Mathew, I fell for you."

She stared at him. Her mouth opened, closed, then opened again. She had no idea what to say. God, he couldn't be serious. Could he?

"True story." He opened the heavy log door to Sid's and gestured for her to enter.

"Oh." She studied his expression. She was flattered, scared, and maybe, just maybe, thrilled by his nonchalant confession. At least until she realized he wasn't so casual. He really meant what he was saying; she could see the truth in his eyes. There was caring there and a hint of fear, too.

"Don't let that scare you. No pressure, no expectations. Just two friends sharing a meal."

She walked past him into the dim interior of the restaurant.

The hostess greeted Clint by name, then led them through a maze of tables to a secluded table in the back. People glanced at them as they passed by. A few greeted Clint by name, but most just nodded at them.

Clint held Natalie's chair until she was seated, and he paid careful attention as the hostess described the evening's specials. Natalie's gaze darted around the room, checking out everyone she could see. There were a lot of strangers, but none of them paid her any attention. Everyone was dressed nicely, and nobody had the thuggish looks of Stanley's goons. Hopefully, there wasn't anyone who'd report back to Stanley. She was getting so tired of living like this, having to mistrust everyone, keeping her eyes open in all directions for strangers.

Eventually, she managed to relax a bit. She was shocked by the ambiance; she hadn't even noticed the hostess walking away. The tables were covered with white linen tablecloths. Floating candle centerpieces lit the room just enough to see clearly. The candlelight reflected from spotless silverware and gleaming wine and water glasses. Apparently, Sid's Steakhouse was an upscale, five-star restaurant; a fact totally hidden by its rough exterior. Sid's was busy, but the conversation was quiet and personal.

"You look surprised." Clint's voice startled her attention back to the table.

"I am." She scanned the room again. "This isn't at all what I was expecting. I mean, I've walked by this place dozens of times on my way to the grocery store." She shook her head.

Clint laughed.

"Come on, it's an old, log building with thick, distorted glass in the windows. I expected the same inside. But it's…elegant." She waved her hand around vaguely.

"Sid's is—or rather was—one of the first buildings in Haven. Have you met Gypsy?"

Natalie nodded.

"Gypsy's family erected this building as a barn. Years later, they added the windows and over time, it was reconditioned for other uses. It's been a mercantile, a gym, a hardware store and now Sid's. Sid took over about six years ago when the hardware store went under. The plate-glass windows were replaced with custom glass to replicate the original, handcrafted glass windows from Gypsy's grandmother's era. The place was shut down for months, then one day, a sign went up for Sid's Steakhouse."

"Wow. That's quite a story. I wouldn't think a steakhouse would survive in a place this small."

"Normally, it wouldn't. In fact, Sid nearly went under several years ago."

"Until," a female voice said, "I opened for breakfast, too."

A tall, reed-thin redhead glided up to their table.

"Breakfast?"

"A girl has to make a living. Frankly, you wouldn't recognize this place in the daytime. No linens. No china. Just bright, florescent lights. It isn't what I intended when I opened, but it works."

"Natalie, meet Sidney James. Sidney, Natalie Schwartz." He introduced them with a wave of his hands.

"Welcome to Haven, Natalie. I hope you enjoy it here," Sid said graciously. She turned to Clint. "I didn't believe it when they told me you had a date here. You don't date."

"Not since you broke my heart." The light tone in his voice told Natalie he was joking.

"Dude, you never stood a chance." Sid smiled at him and turned back to Natalie. "He's totally not my type. Well, duty calls." She gestured toward a patiently waiting server. "Enjoy your dinner. Wine's on the house."

"Not her type?" How could Clint not be her type? He was

attractive, he had a great body and he was kind, generous and successful.

"Definitely not her type." Clint laughed.

Natalie gave him a quizzical look.

"Let's just say…her gate doesn't swing that way." He smiled.

"Her gate?" Natalie pondered the statement, but then it dawned on her. "Oh, her gate. She's gay?"

"You don't have to whisper. It's not a secret. Everyone knows. She's lived with her wife since they opened Sid's. Initially it was quite a shocker for this small town, but people got over it." He tapped her menu. "What do you want for supper? I'm thinking about the steak special."

"There's a steak special?"

"The hostess told us the specials, but you were busy people watching." His voice was teasing, but her face heated anyway.

"Sorry, I was kind of shell-shocked. What are they?"

The waitress arrived, filled their water glasses, poured their wine, recited the specials again, then asked if they wanted anything else to drink while they decided. When she departed, they spent a few minutes enjoying the wine and chatting. Eventually, they both settled on the rib-eye steak special with baked potato, asparagus and grilled mushrooms.

"Tell me about your day."

"I have a job. At the bookstore." Natalie twitched excitedly. "Well, I do if I can find daycare for Mathew."

"That's excellent. Emily has space, and she's great with kids."

"I don't know." She fiddled with her fork. "I've never really left him with anyone before. I worry."

"Didn't he have a nanny before you came here?"

"Yes and no. I hated leaving him with her. Don't get me wrong, Colleen was wonderful. She adored Mathew, and she was good with him, but I rarely used her. She lived in and was always around, but she always deferred to Stanley. Everyone deferred to Stanley."

Bitter memories crept in. She waggled her shoulders to release the tension in her neck.

"That bothered you?"

"Yes, it bothered me. He was an arrogant, controlling, an abusive son-of-a-bitch, and I hate him with every fiber of my being." She clamped a hand over her mouth, surprised as much by her confession as her vehemence. She glanced furtively around the restaurant, but no one paid any attention to them. She breathed a sigh of relief that her outburst had gone unnoticed. "Sorry."

"I wondered about the bruises you had when you arrived. I overheard you tell Doc you were clumsy, but I've never seen a sign of it." Before she could comment, he continued... "And the night I drove you to town, you were absolutely terrified of me. You refused to call your husband after the accident." He ticked points off on his fingers. "You wanted your car out of sight. You showed up dressed in high fashion, but you have no money." He slammed his hand down on the table. "Dammit. I knew someone abused you."

A dozen faces turned, and he faked a smile and waited until they turned their attention back to their own business.

"Tell me the bastard didn't hurt Mathew. I'll kill the son-of-a-bitch if he hit that boy. I should kill him anyway."

When Natalie calmed from his anger, Clint realized how he must sound, especially to someone with her past. He reached out to touch her hand, and she jerked it away.

Slowly, he raised his hands in surrender. He hated the fear in her eyes, and the defensive hunching of her shoulders.

"I'm sorry, Natalie. I didn't mean to scare you. No man should ever hurt a child or a woman. A real man doesn't use violence to solve problems." He saw the disbelief in her eyes.

"I mean it, Natalie. I apologize. I kind of lost my cool there."

He sighed and lowered his hands. "You have nothing to fear from me. Ever."

Natalie slowly pushed her chair back and stood. "Goodnight, Clint." She took a slow, careful step backward.

"Wait." He didn't move except to gesture to her chair. "Please stay."

"I…I don't think so." Her gaze darted wildly around the room.

"Please. I don't deserve it, but please give me one more chance."

Natalie backed away another step.

"My birthfather beat my mother, nearly to death, when he found out she was pregnant with me." His eyes pleaded with her. "He left her for dead and went back to his wife."

Natalie's hand flew up to her throat. "No."

"Yes. She told me he wasn't a good man when I was in my teens. She thought I was old enough then to understand why he wasn't part of our life." Emboldened by Natalie's small step forward, he went on. "I've never told anyone this. When she died, she left me a letter telling me who I was and who the rich bastard who fathered me was. She told me to find him and demand my share of his wealth."

Clint smiled encouragingly when Natalie eased back into her seat. She didn't comment and still appeared ready to bolt, but her eyes were filled with compassion.

"I met him. He was an arrogant, self-inflated asshole. I hated him with a passion. I walked away from him and his money and never looked back. Hell, he could be dead for all I know." He looked at his hands where they rested on the table, palms up. Silently, he renewed his vow. No matter what, his hands would never harm a woman.

Slowly, hesitantly, Natalie reached out and placed her hand on Clint's upturned palm. "I'm sorry you lived through that."

Clint looked up. A lone tear streamed down her face. He lifted his other hand slowly and wiped it away.

"Don't be sad for me. I was never beaten. My mother loved me until her dying day. I was better off without him."

"Oh, Clint." Natalie stroked his palm softly.

"Here you go." Sid placed their plates in front of them. She looked back and forth between them. "Is everything okay?" She gave Natalie an understanding look.

Natalie nodded. She swallowed hard. "Fine," she managed to croak at last.

"Will you stay?" Clint ignored Sid.

"I'll stay." Natalie pulled her chair closer to the table. "Thank you, Sid. Everything is fine."

Sid gave Clint a warning glare, smiled reassuringly at Natalie, nodded, then walked away.

~

"I'M NOT sure I can eat." Natalie stared at her plate for a minute. "The food looks delicious, though."

"It does, but I'm not sure I can eat, either. But we have to try, or Sid will be all over me, demanding explanations for the wasted food and wanting to know what I did to you. She gets kind of protective sometimes." He smiled wryly and picked up his fork.

"Protective? She doesn't even know me, and I thought she'd smack you when she walked up." She looked around the restaurant for Sid, who stood by the bar staring at them. Natalie gave her a small reassuring wave and turned back to Clint.

"She's glaring at us." Natalie smoothed her napkin on her lap.

Clint glanced over his shoulder at the restauranteur. "No, she's glaring at me. As well she should. I hurt you with my words. I owe you an apology."

"No, you don't. I can be…timid. I'm afraid it's a long-engrained habit." She forced herself to take a bite of her potato, then one of her asparagus and swallowed. "My father never hit me, but he was controlling, all the same. I never knew my mother. She died when I was very young. I married Stanley under duress. Mathew was the only good thing to come from my marriage. I've lived a timid, overly controlled life of luxury. Well, luxury until I arrived here. Haven has been an adjustment for me. But I'm learning to stand on my own two feet and to stand up for myself. I had to cut and run from my marriage. He doesn't know where I am, only that I'm gone. I don't want him to find me. Ever."

Clint opened his mouth to speak, but she forestalled his words with a curt gesture.

"Let me finish. This isn't easy."

He nodded.

"You scared me. Abuse has been my norm for too long, and I refuse to accept it again. So, I was leaving. But I may have been wrong. I don't think you meant to frighten me or to hurt me, but your anger scares me." She closed her eyes and forced herself to breathe deeply after her confession. It was frightening and liberating, all at once.

"God. You've been through so much. So much more than I ever imagined. I'm so sorry I frightened you. I can't say enough how sorry I am." He looked her in the eyes. "But I promise you this, no matter how angry I am at you or at anyone or anything else, I will never hit you or Mathew."

He swallowed deeply, as if he were swallowing a lump in his throat. He looked so apologetic, so sincere.

"And if you never want to see me again, I understand. I won't like it, but I'll stay away. I swear to you, on my mother's grave."

He dropped his fork, swallowed and blinked a couple times. Was he holding back a tear? Natalie gave a mental head shake. No, it couldn't be. She studied him long and hard. Looking for the truth, searching for signs of deception and failing to find any.

She held out her hand. "Hi. I'm Natalie Schwartz." Maybe, they could make a fresh start now with all their cards on the table. "I'm not looking for a relationship, but I could use a friend."

He took her hand and shook it firmly but gently. "Clinton

James Dawson. It's nice to meet you, Natalie." He released her hand slowly and picked up his fork.

"So, Clint, tell me a bit about yourself." Natalie cut into her steak.

He looked thoughtful for a moment. "I've lived in Haven for six years. After my mother passed away, I rambled around a bit and eventually landed here when I took a job with the Forest Service for the summer. Seasonal work. I was thinking about going to the university in the fall, but I never really got around to applying. I liked it here. There's something special about the mountains in the summer."

"It is beautiful here."

"And I have to admit, I'd gotten used to Haven. I rented the trailer you live in from Paul Timber. He owned the garage then. He's retired now. Spends most of his time fishing at Lost Lake. I got lucky. I was out of work, out of money and Paul was short-handed because a bunch of his staff had managed to be accepted at a university or college. Unlike me."

"That was lucky for you." How many people ended up in Haven by chance?

"Turns out I'm a pretty damned, er danged, good mechanic. Eventually, Paul sold me the garage, café, convenience store, campground and trailer." He shrugged. "It wasn't my intention to end up here. Heck, I don't even know if I had any intentions back then. At twenty-eight, I had no idea what I'd do with my life. I'd worked in a lot of jobs. I was kind of a jack of all trades after high school. Mom had been sick for years. Self-employed, spotty work allowed me the freedom to help her out."

"That was generous of you. I'm sure you gave her a lot of good years. You didn't have to do that." Such selflessness had once been a foreign concept to Natalie, but recently, she'd learned it was more common than she'd ever expected. She was surprised Clint blushed.

"It's nothing compared to what she gave me. She worked through her entire pregnancy, ran a daycare until I started school, then did shift work until I graduated high school." He smiled fondly. "God, she was hard on me when I slacked off." He laughed. "She used to say, and I quote, 'Clinton, get your lazy ass off that couch and do your homework. Ain't no son of mine going to be a useless lay about. You need an education.' I resented the hell out of her for a while. But eventually, her words sank in. I just wish she'd been alive to see me change."

"You don't think she saw it, while she was sick? When you devoted your life to taking care of her?" Natalie paused. "She knew," she said with certainty. "I'll bet she's looking down on you now, pleased as punch at how you've turned out. You're a good man, Clinton Dawson." Natalie patted his hand comfortingly.

He blushed again. "Enough about me. Tell me a bit about you. How did you end up in Haven?"

For a moment, she hesitated to answer him. It was a touchy subject, but he already knew the truth, so she put a humorous spin on it. "I stole a car and crashed it in the bush, and a handsome man rescued me." She laughed. "He claims to be a pretty good mechanic, but he's not particularly efficient."

"Maybe, he's busy."

"Maybe, he keeps making excuses to check on me." She took a nibble of her potato.

"Perhaps, he's worried or smitten."

Natalie laughed and glanced at her plate to avoid his penetrating gaze. She was surprised to discover she'd almost finished her meal. "Or he's an incorrigible flirt."

"I have it on good authority he's a fine, upstanding citizen who works hard and cares for his friends." Clint gave her a devious look.

"Oh, you." Natalie couldn't resist his teasing smile and found her own growing. "I am grateful for everything you've done for us."

"I've been happy to help out."

Laying her silverware across her plate, she gave him an assessing look. He met her gaze and held it for several long moments.

"You actually mean that, don't you?"

"I do. I don't have much use for selfish people." He shook his head. "I believe in helping out when I can."

"Well, I do appreciate it, and I know I've needed a lot of help." She looked away.

"That's the way it goes. Sometimes, you need help; sometimes, you give help. It's a two-way street."

"Sadly, I've been on the receiving end way too often. It isn't a place I'm comfortable with. Although, it does seem to be a habit lately." She fiddled with her napkin, wiped her mouth, then took a slow drink of water.

"You've been on the giving end, too."

"No, I haven't."

"Yes, you have. You've done my laundry, my mending—"

"You've given me a place to stay for my work, so it isn't a favor. At least, not a favor to you."

"Tell my formerly button-less shirts that." He laughed. "And you've babysat for Grace and for Lisa. You've helped Harmony weed her garden, and you've done other things, as well."

She looked at him in surprise. "I did, didn't I? I never looked at it like that. I thought I was just taking." She heard the smile in her voice. She was pleased to think she was…useful.

"I wasn't sure about you at first."

She looked at him. "What does that mean?" She scrunched up her nose, considering.

"Don't take this the wrong way…"

"Something tells me I'm not going to like this."

"When I first saw you at the bottom of that hill, dripping wet, struggling to bring Mathew to safety, I was struck by your determination. Then, when I brought up your bags and did your laundry, all I saw was the immense money you put into clothing yourself. You seemed so lost, so helpless. I thought maybe you were one of the useless idle rich, depending on everyone else instead of doing for yourself." His words were hesitant, thoughtful.

"Ouch." Natalie winced. "But—"

She didn't get to finish her thought before Clint interrupted. "Don't get me wrong."

"There's only one way to take that."

"I'm not finished." He pushed on before she could say anything. "Then I watched you with Mathew. You could barely walk, yet you cared for him. Without complaint. You stood up for yourself and tried to be self-sufficient. Hell, you didn't even want help from me. You couldn't wait to be out of my hair and away from me."

She was silent for a long time, grateful he let her think. *This is it. He's done with me. He knows who or rather what I really am.* She crossed her arms and rubbed away the chill that enveloped her.

"You were right. No, make that you are right. I am the useless, idle-rich." She held up a hand to stop the objection she could see forming. "At least, that was me. I did nothing for myself, except caring for Mathew. But I've learned to stand on my feet. I don't have people catering to my every whim anymore. And I like it. I like figuring things out, choosing where to go, what to do and how to do it." She smiled proudly. "I like the new me."

She didn't give him a chance to speak. "I still don't know how I'm going to make it without Stanley, but at least, I know now I can make it."

"It's a big change."

"You think I don't know that?" She grinned and gave him a self-mocking laugh. "I have no money, no car, and I'm about to start my first job ever. I'm scared to death and exhilarated all at once. For the first time in my life, I think I can handle just about anything. And I owe it all to you for helping me find my feet." She clasped his hand between hers and squeezed gently. "I owe you, big time."

"You don't owe me anything. Now, how about dessert?"

"Dessert?" She waved at her empty plate. "I've already eaten more tonight than I have all week."

"And that is precisely why you need dessert. So, what'll it be?

Five-layer chocolate cake, cheesecake, crème brûlée, apple pie or the mousse sampler?"

"You have the dessert menu memorized?"

"I'm kind of a dessert guy." He looked around for their server.

"Is there anything lighter?" She didn't know why she'd asked. She certainly didn't need anything else to eat, but to prolong the evening that had turned from ugly to surprisingly pleasant, she might be convinced to eat a bit more.

"Well, there's a fruit and cheese plate, but that's not dessert." He wrinkled his nose in disgust.

The waitress glided in and silently removed their plates, leaving a dessert menu in their place.

"I think I'll pass on dessert."

"I'm going to have the chocolate cake." Clint rubbed his hands together. "It's the biggest dessert on the menu."

"How can you be hungry?"

"I'm a man. I need more food than a mere woman. Besides, I work hard. Automotive work can be physical, depending on what you're doing. Today, I was pulling an overturned rig out of the same ditch you went into on Clive's Corner. Remind me, I have your shoes. I found them in the ditch. They're a little worse for wear, but they might be functional." He shrugged as if to indicate he didn't know much about women's footwear.

"Thanks. I hope the driver wasn't hurt."

"He's fine, but the shoes do bring up a question." He left the statement open ended, leaving her a chance to ignore it.

"And that is?"

"Why the hell did you run off in stilettos? Wouldn't sneakers have made more sense? Flats of some kind? Sandals?"

"I wasn't thinking straight. When Stanley fell and hit his head, I grabbed Mathew and bolted—after I made sure he was breathing."

"I'm curious as to why you didn't leave before that."

"You sure go for the jugular. I'm not sure I'm ready to get into all that." She wanted to drop the subject. She abhorred talking about Stanley. She just wanted to be free of that part of her life.

"How about dessert?" She grasped the menu and flipped it open. She knew he wasn't fooled by her sudden interest, but was grateful when he didn't pursue the topic.

"Here you go." Sid slid a sampler platter of desserts between them. The plate held small pieces of each of the restaurant's desserts and a larger slice of the daily dessert, stacked strawberry shortcake. "I thought you might like something sweet to finish your meal." The smile she gave Clint was mocking. She turned to Natalie. "Was your meal okay?" Her look conveyed her double meaning.

"My steak was perfect. It melted in my mouth. It was an excellent dinner." She gave Sid a smile. "Thank you for asking."

"Dinner was great, as always. And after an initial screw up, I stopped being a jerk."

"Good thing, too." Sid shook her finger at him. "I thought I'd have to kick your ass." She thanked them for coming, then left them to their dessert.

Dessert was fabulous. Each item was perfection, but Natalie's favorite was the strawberry shortcake. Four layers of moist white cake separated by layers of whipped cream, fresh strawberries in a gelee sauce and topped with more whipped cream and fresh whole strawberries dipped in white chocolate.

"That was so much more than I needed." Natalie patted her full tummy. "But that shortcake," she scooped up the last of the whipped cream and savored it, "was decadent. I may never eat again."

"How about an after-dinner drink?"

"How about you roll me home and tuck me in bed?" Her eyes widened. "Um, that isn't what I meant."

"Perhaps, a slow walk around town to burn off all that food," he suggested. "Even I have to admit, I'm stuffed to the gills." He quickly settled the check, helped her into her sweater, then before she realized it, they were strolling down Main Street.

Night was falling, and the air was cool as it whispered across her skin and through her hair. Natalie inhaled deeply. "I love the piney scent of the air here. It's so different than in the city."

"You wouldn't have liked it a few years ago. They were selectively logging a couple valleys over and had a sawmill set up. There's nothing worse than the acid stench of a sawmill. It burns the lining from your nose and penetrates everything."

"Ew. I smelled that once when I lived in BC. I'm glad I missed it." Her nose wrinkled at the memory. "You know what else I like?" Without waiting for him to comment she went on. "The stars here. They're so much bigger and brighter. I feel like I can reach out and touch them."

"That's because—"

"Don't you dare interrupt this moment with a scientific explanation. Haven't you got any romance in your soul?" She gave him a mock glare. "Look around. The night sky, the full moon, the stars and the old-fashioned streetlights. They look like antique gas lamps. The houses have neat yards and picket fences. The air is fresh and clean."

"I've enjoyed a nice dinner with a wonderful, intriguing woman."

"Don't go there, please." She distanced herself.

Without another word, he took her small, soft hand into his large calloused one and walked on. She hesitated, with a bit of a stumble, then decided to let it go. They walked along wordlessly, up and down the streets, touring slowly, taking in the night sounds and sights until at last, over an hour later, he led her up the path to her gate.

"I'm going to say goodnight here." He cupped her chin in his hand and tilted her face toward him.

Her breath caught in her throat as she looked into his eyes. He was so handsome, so kind, and he was going to kiss her. She knew it. She should turn away. But she didn't. She froze. Waiting. And waiting some more, her heart pounding, her pulse racing. Finally, when she thought she couldn't last another second, he brushed his thumb across her lips, whispered goodnight and walked away.

She stood motionless, watching him until he disappeared in the trees at the end of the park. Her fingers pressed gently to her tingling lips.

"Oh my."

The soft sound of a door closing, followed by footsteps, came from behind her. Lisa.

"He didn't even kiss you goodnight." Lisa's voice was filled with awe.

Natalie shook her head mutely, still half-transfixed by his action.

"Dinner was good?"

Nat nodded.

"I'll just go, then."

Nat nodded again as Lisa walked away. Belatedly, she called out after her. "Thanks for looking after Mathew."

Lisa laughed and waved. "Anytime, my friend. Anytime."

CHAPTER 14

*N*atalie paused on the front step of Emily's house. Children's music and the sounds of youngsters singing came from inside. It sounded chaotic. How could she leave Mathew here and go off to work? She was his mother. He needed her.

She stood there, frozen with indecision. She was out of options, and she knew it. She had no money; she needed to work to feed them, or she'd have to go back to Stanley.

The sound of a screaming, angry child penetrated the morning. How could she leave Mathew here?

Before Natalie could convince her feet to move, Emily dealt with the child, her voice kind and calm. "Sasha, you have to share with Amy. That's what we do. We let everyone play with the toys."

"But it's mine. I had it first." Sasha sounded petulant.

"Remember, Sasha," Emily said patiently, "the toys are for everyone. That's why you don't bring your toys here. Your dolls are at home. This doll is my doll. Please give Amy a turn."

"I don't wanna," Sasha pouted.

"We have two choices, ladies," Emily said. "Sasha, you and Amy can share the dolls or we'll have to pick them up and put them on the shelf for another day." The muted sound of shifting toys filtered through the window.

"Here you go. Look, I found three dolls. Which one would you like, Sasha?" After a mumbled reply by the child, Emily said, "and which one would you like, Amy?" Again there was a mumble. "See, girls. That was easy. Now, we'll just put the extra doll over here, and you can both play. I see a couple blankets and toy bottles over there." For a moment there was silence, then the sound of two small, girlie voices playing mother.

"Mommy, I don't wanna play dollies." Mathew tugged at Natalie's hand.

"Don't worry, Sweetie. Miss Emily won't make you play dolls. Remember when we came over the other day? You played trucks and colored and had a snack. Miss Emily has lots of things for you to do."

The front door opened, and Emily stepped outside, closing the door on the now-happy chaos inside. "Hi. I'm glad you came. I was worried you might have second thoughts." She waved toward the house. "Luckily, those moments are rare around here. Distraction is usually the solution." She smiled matter-of-factly.

"Okay, Mathew." Natalie knelt down to look him in the eyes. "Remember what we talked about. I'm going to the bookstore. You'll stay here with the kids and Miss Emily for a while and then I'll come back."

"No." He crossed his arms across his chest and stared at the ground.

"Yes." Natalie hugged him tightly. "Mommy has to go to work now."

"But you never workded before." His arms snaked around her neck and pulled her closer.

"I never needed to before. But now, Mommy needs to work so we can stay in Haven, so you can play with your friends."

"Come inside, Mathew." Emily opened the door. "You can help me make popcorn for our snack."

"Popcorn?" He wiggled out of Natalie's arms and bolted for the door.

"I'll call you at the store if there's an issue," Emily reassured Natalie. "I've got this." She touched Natalie gently on the arm and smiled.

"I know. It's just…hard." Natalie sighed. Then she reminded herself what was at stake. It was either life with Stanley's abuse, or peace and relative safety here in Haven. She took a step away. "Bye, Mathew. Thanks, Emily." Reluctantly, she walked away from him. It almost killed her not to look back and ensure he was okay. She listened for his voice, waiting for him to call her back. Disappointment that he didn't make an appeal battled with relief he was okay with her leaving. Parenting was way more difficult than she'd ever imagined.

It was nearly one-thirty before she had time to think about Mathew again. The bookstore was insane. It was the first official weekend of tourist season, and the place was jumping. Tourists mingled with locals, all hoping to find some bargains in Grace's first sale of the season.

Natalie split her time between serving in the coffee area, working the floor and helping customers find things, and learning to run the computer sales program. She made a few errors but was catching on quickly to what was expected of her. She was pleasantly surprised at how useful her wide, eclectic reading tastes turned out to be.

"You're doing great." Grace held the door open for Natalie, and they stepped out onto the staff-only deck that ran the length of the back of the store, separating it from the parking lot. The shade was a welcome respite from the heat of the bookstore. The air conditioner was on, but with so many people coming in and out of the store, it was having trouble keeping the temperature lower. She poured Natalie a frosty glass of frozen lemonade from the pitcher on the side table.

"Thanks." Natalie took a long, slow drink. "Oh, this is so nice."

She leaned against a pillar and let the breeze wash over her. "I think I'm getting the hang of the job." She looked at Grace for agreement.

"You catch on quick, and you're doing well. Although, I thought that guy would faint when his books rang up to fifty grand."

"Oh man. I was so embarrassed. I'm glad you were there to help me out." She laughed at her own ineptitude.

"Not half as glad as he was." They laughed together. "Mistakes like that are easy to fix, so, no worries."

"What's so funny?" Clint strode through the back door onto the deck. He smiled at them both, but his gaze lingered on the length of Natalie's legs, where they peeked demurely from beneath her knee-length skirt.

They shared the story with him, and he laughed, too. "Remind me not to let you sell me anything." He winked at Natalie.

"What are you doing here in the middle of the day?" Grace slyly looked from Clint to Natalie. "As if I didn't already know."

"I just stopped by to tell Nat, Mathew is doing great. Emily has everyone settled down for quiet time."

"He's doing okay?"

"He had a minor meltdown over some building blocks. But nothing serious. I knew you'd be too busy to get away and check on him, so I did it for you."

Natalie leaned over and gave him a kiss on the cheek. "That's so sweet of you." She blushed at her boldness.

"I live to please." Clint bowed. "Well, gotta run. I've got a truckload of work today." He tipped an imaginary hat at Grace and pecked Natalie on the mouth before leaping over the railing to the parking lot. "I'll be by around six with dinner." He waved over his shoulder as he strolled away.

They watched him go.

"By that, I assume he means for you." Grace snickered. "Because, he's never offered to feed me."

Natalie gaped at her, shocked.

"Close your mouth, girl. He likes you. It's not that surprising."

"I hardly know him."

"Oh, don't give me that old song and dance." Grace swatted Natalie playfully on the elbow. "You've been here for a while now. You see him virtually every day. You know he's a good man. He's good with your son. You do Clint's laundry. You wash his underwear, for Pete's sake. How much do you need to know? It's not like you're going to marry him." She flashed a knowing glance at Natalie's wedding rings.

"I'm already married." Natalie looked down, avoiding her friend's eyes.

"So you say," Grace said, taking a deep breath. "I see the ring. I hear the declaration. I've never seen your husband, but I've witnessed the bruises. Why don't you divorce him? Move on with your life?"

"It isn't that simple. I can't go back to him, to that life. I'm not who I was then. It's…complicated." She dropped into a chair, trying to relax.

"Love always is." Grace was serious, but joking, too.

"I'm not in love with Stanley. I never was."

"I wasn't talking about your ex, assuming that's who Stanley is. I was talking about Clint." She touched Natalie's shoulder gently. "Look, I'm not going to pry. But take my word for it. Running from your troubles doesn't solve them. It only delays confrontation or, in your case, love."

"It's not that easy." Natalie sighed and fiddled with her glass, wiping away the condensation clouding its outside.

"Explain it to me. Sometimes, having someone to talk to, to vent to, helps ease the burden. It isn't good to keep things bottled up inside. It makes you tense, brittle and on edge. Sooner or later, Mathew is going to wonder what's going on and why he doesn't see his father. Assuming he knows his father."

"He knows him. I just wish he didn't." Natalie hugged herself tightly and squirmed in her chair. "My husband isn't a nice man. I never should have married him."

"Why did you marry him?"

"I wanted to make my father happy. Lord knows, I could never live up to his expectations. I was always too stupid, too much of a girl, not good enough, not refined enough. I didn't want the marriage. God, I've never liked Stanley. Something about him always bothered me." Once the words started flowing, she couldn't stop them. "He was always angry when he drank, but not once during our so-called courtship did he show any violent tendencies. The mental and physical abuse started after we were married.

"I should have been stronger and gone with my instincts, but I never could say no to my father. When he pressed for marriage, I gave in, hoping to please him. Just once, I wanted him to be proud of me." She fell silent, her eyes closed. "His support and fatherly convictions were offered for about a month, until the first time Stanley told him I'd screwed up. It was as if my inability to please my father reset and started again." She looked at Grace, her eyes pleading for understanding. She didn't know why she needed validation, but she wanted Grace to grasp what had motivated her.

"What could you have done that was so terrible?"

Natalie leapt to her feet. "I tripped. I frigging tripped." For the first time in her life, she didn't care she was cursing. "I tripped on a cord and spilled a glass of red wine on myself, but more damaging, on a white Persian rug."

"Who doesn't spill stuff?" Grace appeared confused. "And why was it a big deal?"

"Women with class and grace don't spill things." Natalie mimicked her husband's sanctimonious attitude. "Only fat cows like me are graceless and uncouth."

"Jesus, girl. You're not fat. You're not even plump. Hell, you barely make curvy. You're beautiful, and I've never seen you do anything graceless or uncoordinated in all the time you've been in Haven. Why would he say something like that?" Her voice was sharp with anger and recrimination. "And why the hell would he tell your father?"

Tears slipped down Natalie's cheeks. "On the day of my wedding, I overheard my father thanking him for taking on the burden of turning me into someone worthy of my heritage. I didn't find out until my father died that they had a…a…a business deal. Stanley would civilize me in exchange for becoming my father's sole heir."

"Civilize you? Are you kidding? You're the most refined woman I know."

"No, I'm not. I'm chunky, crude and rough around the edges." Natalie snatched up her glass and swilled the rest of her lemonade.

"I'm going to let that go. There are too many things wrong with that statement to even start fixing it. You are none of those things. So, he married you for money?"

Natalie shivered at the memory. "And he was paid well for it, too. When my father died, Stanley inherited almost thirty billion dollars. He didn't need the money. His family is well off. He has a huge, successful company. My father screwed me over and gave everything to a man who already had more than he needed." Her words felt circular and not quite clear. "And I had to beg for every dollar I spent. Except for the clothing Stanley chose for me."

"Your father gave him everything? He didn't leave you anything?"

"Not one fucking red cent." Natalie moaned and paced the small confines of the deck. "God, I hate them both."

"So, divorce him. Walk away."

"I can't. Mathew is his son. How can I, a single mother who only started her first job and is living on someone else's charity, get custody of Mathew? Stanley has half the judges and politicians in Vancouver in his back pocket. He's got money to burn. No judge, corrupt or not, would ever give me custody. I'd never see Mathew again." She straightened her shoulders and looked Grace square in the eye. "And there's no damn way I'm going to let that abusive bastard get his filthy hands on Mathew. If I have to run for the rest of my life, I will never, ever, let him near Mathew." Her hands trembled with tension as she rubbed her neck.

After a deep breath to restore her mental equilibrium, she went on, "I may have to run and hide, but Mathew will never know abuse. He'll always know how special he is and how much I love him. We may not have money, but he'll always know love." She wiped the tears off her face with the backs of her hands and turned to go inside. At the threshold, she paused. "Please, don't tell anyone about me. I need to keep hidden."

"I won't breathe a word." Grace stepped toward Natalie and hugged her tightly. "But you should think about filing for divorce and filing a restraining order. You need to break free."

"I need to be alone for a moment. Please excuse me." Natalie stepped back inside the store.

~

GRACE SAT IN A DECK CHAIR. "There has to be something I can do."

"Something *we* can do." Clint stepped around the corner.

"Shit. You didn't hear anything." She pressed her finger to her lips.

"I couldn't help but hear. I was on my way back to see if Mathew liked fish, and I heard you ask why Natalie married that —" Guilt battered at him. He should have made a sound or something.

"Why didn't you let us know you were here?" Her glare could have sliced a lesser man to ribbons.

"I had to know. I had to know what made those shadows beneath her eyes. What makes her skittish and afraid. Come on, Grace, you would have listened, too." He gestured helplessly and stepped onto the deck.

"Dammit, Clint, you aren't like that. You don't eavesdrop." Her words were an accusation and a question. "How much did you hear?"

"I heard every word, but until she tells me herself, I won't let on that I know. And I'll find some way to help her through this. She needs to be free of the worry that he'll chase her down."

"And her husband's money?"

"I'm not interested in that. Have you ever known me to care about money?" Clint countered. "I'm comfortable. You know that. This is about Natalie. And Mathew. They're two good people trapped in an ugly situation. And I intend to help them." He slouched into a chair. "I don't even care if she doesn't want anything to do with me."

"Sure, sure." Grace laughed at his lie.

"Okay, maybe, I do care. I'll tell you something and if you ever tell her, I'll deny it." He waited for her nod before he went on. "I like Natalie. Hell, I might even love her. All I want is for her to be happy. Mathew is like a son to me already. But if she doesn't want me…" He shrugged sadly. "As long as she's happy and safe."

Grace smiled. "I always knew you were a good man."

LATER THAT AFTERNOON, Clint stood in the garage, staring blankly at the car he was working on. He didn't notice the other mechanic working in the next bay. Dimly, he was aware of the clanging of tools on metal car parts and the ding of the gas hose outside. Something nagged at him. It tickled at the edge of his mind. Natalie's words circled through his mind over and over again, almost triggering a thought process. He couldn't shake the feeling something important lay just outside his reach. But, for the life of him, he couldn't quite put his finger on it.

"What's up, boss?" Tim, Clint's apprentice mechanic, startled Clint back to the present.

"Just thinking."

"Doesn't look that complicated." Tim waved at the car. "She needs a new oil pan and a gasket."

"What?"

"The car." He nodded toward the car on the hoist. "That's why she's here."

Clint had to laugh at himself. "I wasn't thinking about the car. I've got stuff on my mind."

"Stuff? Don't you mean a woman?" The youth laughed. "You've been drooling over her since she arrived. You've disappeared more times this month than since I started pumping gas for you four years ago." He flexed his eyebrows suggestively. "Dude, I've never seen you gooey eyed over a woman. Besides, she's married. You told me that yourself. When I was interested in Andrea and she was dating Steve, you told me to back off. Never chase another man's woman. You've seen those rocks she wears. Don't go there. I don't know where her husband is, but married chicks are bad news."

His words echoed in Clint's mind. Where was Natalie's husband? Who was he? Stanley. He had a sick feeling he had an idea who Stanley might be, and if he was right, it was a huge coincidence and it wasn't good. Not good at all. Just thinking about it made him feel nauseous. He became lightheaded, and his heart stuttered. He leaned heavily on the car.

"Crap man, you're as white as a sheet." Tim reached out to grasp Clint by the shoulder. "You sick?"

"Not sick, worried. I've got to run. Keep an eye on things. Call my cell if you need me," Clint blurted, heading for the door.

"Dude, I told you not to go there."

Clint heard the words but didn't pause; he just kept going.

If Stanley was who Clint thought he was, this could get ugly in a hurry, really ugly. There was one sure way to find out. If Natalie knew what he was about to do, she'd kill him. But he had to know the truth before the situation got any further out of hand.

CHAPTER 15

*A*lisha stared at the stick in her hand.

A pink plus sign.

This wasn't good. It wasn't good at all. She became lightheaded and wobbled unsteadily on her feet before dropping to her knees.

It had been two months since she'd last seen Stanley. Her ribs were finally healing from his kick. She didn't want this, not now. Not ever. Once, she'd thought she loved him or maybe just his money and what he could offer her. Back then, she would have welcomed his child as a way into his world. Now, she just wanted him gone. She wanted to forget she'd ever known him.

"Fuck." She pitched the test strip into the bathroom trash. A wave of revulsion and nausea washed over her, and she gagged and lurched forward, barely hitting the toilet with the contents of her stomach. So much for breakfast.

After washing up, brushing her teeth and throwing on some clean clothes, she made her way to the couch. What the hell was she going to do now? She didn't want his brat.

Did she?

She rolled the possibilities around in her head. Baby or no baby?

Could she raise a child? Did she want to? How could she afford it? She'd only just started her new job after Stanley had fired her. There was no way she could raise a baby and work fulltime.

"Women do it all the time." Saying the words aloud didn't quell the rising panic.

"I do not want *this* baby." She swore a blue streak. "He isn't the child of love."

What if it's a girl? Her thoughts raced back to her unhappy childhood. Living a life of near poverty with her addicted, prostitute mother. Being forced to service her mother's clients until she was old enough to break away on her own. She'd skimmed through the university, *barely*, only surviving by working as a stripper.

She couldn't do that to a child.

Stanley has plenty of money. The guy is a freaking quad-zillionaire.

Did she dare approach him? She could demand money for an abortion and to buy her silence on his infidelity. He was always prattling on about his heir. Maybe, he wanted another one. She could demand money, then give him the brat for his wife to raise.

It dawned on her she couldn't do that to another human being. She couldn't put an innocent into the hands of a monster like Stanley.

"What the fuck am I going to do?" she screamed at the ceiling. "Holy mother fucking cock sucking shit. What am I going to do?" She leapt to her feet and paced the tiny confines of her one-bedroom apartment. God, she missed the luxury of the three-bedroom suite Stanley had rented for her. She hated this little fucking shit box of an apartment. She hated her entire freaking life. She wished she'd never been born.

She wished Stanley was dead.

Slipping into a corner between two tottering piles of unpacked boxes, she slid to the floor, whimpering. Tears flowed down her cheeks and dripped off her chin. She hugged her knees to her chest. What would she do? How had her life gone so colossally wrong?

Hours later, she struggled to her feet. Her head pounded from crying, her legs were stiff and her butt ached from sitting cramped on the floor. But she'd made a decision. She would convince Stanley to give her the money for an abortion by threatening to go to the press with her story. He would want the baby; she knew that. He was all about his fortune and keeping it in the family. She wouldn't subject a child to the abusive side he'd shown her. She'd rather terminate the pregnancy than force a child into a life of abuse.

Thinking about ending the baby's life made her nausea resurface. She gagged and swallowed. There was no way she'd allow Stanley to have access to a child. She'd found a way around that. She'd tell him it was deformed. Stanley would accept nothing but perfection from his family, so he'd give her the money. The parasite in her womb would be gone, and she'd be free to get on with her life.

She hopped into the shower and formulated a plan to corner him on his yacht.

CHAPTER 16

Natalie worked her way through the busy café attached to Clint's gas station, proceeding to the office at the back of the building. She saw Clint through the door, and she needed to talk to him. The closer she got, the slower she moved. She wasn't sure what was slowing her down. Was it the delectable sight of him? A masculine stance that she wanted to enjoy, or the unease she felt in asking for such a big favor.

He didn't appear to notice her coming. He kept typing on his computer keyboard. His gaze traveled from the papers on his desk to the monitor. Back and forth; paper, computer, paper. He was deeply involved in something. He flipped over a paper, entered something then flipped again.

She leaned against the doorjamb without saying anything, just taking a moment to enjoy the sight. There was a slight furrow on his brow as he worked. He didn't seem serious. He just appeared focused. He ran one long, tanned finger down the stark white page, and she wondered what it would be like to feel those fingers running down her skin.

His hands were rough from working with them, but they'd be

149

gentle as they skimmed along her skin. Exploring. Learning her curves. Loving her.

She forced the thought away and studied his face. His brow scrunched further in concentration, and he muttered unrecognizable words. An almost uncontrollable urge to stroke the tension from his brow made her fingers twitch. It was easy to imagine standing behind him, massaging his shoulders and helping him unwind. She watched him working for several minutes before he looked up at her.

"Hi." A large, welcoming grin replaced his frown of concentration. "I didn't hear you. I didn't ignore you for too long, did I? Accounting requires all my attention. If I don't focus, I screw it up."

"I just got here." She fell silent, not sure how to ask for another favor. Instead, she just looked at him, drinking in the sight, sitting there smiling, happy to be with him.

"I like your hair like that." He waved toward her messy up-do then pushed a few keys and shoved the keyboard aside.

He sounded as if he actually meant it, and she smiled, despite knowing stray bits were hanging down. Her hair wasn't long enough to stay in a bun yet, but the early September day was blistering hot, and she couldn't stand having the layers hang heavy and limp on her neck. It was untidy and ratty, but she forced herself not to fret over it.

"Thanks." She wasn't sure how to take the offhand compliment. Stanley had never been one to praise. He'd always preferred to find flaws and point them out.

"Seriously," he said, as if reading her doubt. "I like it. It looks… sexy and relaxed. It makes me want to touch it." He looked as if he wanted to say something else, but instead, he changed the subject. "What can I do for you? You've never come to my office before, and I can count on one hand the number of times you've called. What's up?"

Here goes nothing. "I need a favor."

Clint laughed lightly. "I figured that. You showed up here

unannounced. I thought you were working today. Where's Mathew?"

"I dropped him off at daycare early and came over." A guilty frown turned the corners of her mouth down slightly.

"He'll be fine. Don't fret about him."

"I know, but old habits die hard. Until recently, he only had a sitter if I had no other option. His nanny was overpaid and under-worked." She smiled at the irony. "I've always hated leaving him with someone else." She lowered her gaze then looked back at him. Darn, he had the nicest eyes. Their dark hazel color drew her in until she leaned closer. What would it be like to look in those eyes while he kissed her?

"What? You have the strangest expression on your face. Are you okay?" He was around the desk in a shot.

His hand cupped her shoulder reassuringly. The touch steadied her and brought her errant thoughts back to the present. At the same time, it made her shiver with longing.

"Are you cold? Sick? Do you need a ride to the doctor?"

Natalie shook her head to clear it. "No, I'm fine." She turned to walk away. "I have to go."

Clint's grip on her shoulder tightened. "Wait. You didn't tell me why you came."

"Oh. Yeah." She turned back toward him, drawing a couple steadying breaths. Why was it so hard to ask for help? She could organize a fundraiser, plan and host a dinner party for fifty people and hold her own with the richest people in Vancouver, but she couldn't choke out one simple request. She looked at Clint, who waited patiently for her to speak. His soft, understanding expression helped her find the words.

"I need to borrow a car for a couple days." The words exploded from her mouth.

"Sure. You can use mine. Mind if I ask why?"

Damn. She should have anticipated that question. A person

certainly didn't need a car to get around Haven, except when it was pouring rain.

"Um. Er. I have to go out of town overnight. I need to do something. Mathew is going to stay with Grace."

"Everything okay? Is there anything I can help with? I'm at your disposal." He trailed his fingers down her arm and grasped her hand.

Damn, his hand felt so good. Warm, rough, tender. "No. Thanks. I have to do this by myself," she said carefully, worried her statement might sound dismissive or illusive.

He gave her a quizzical look. "If you're sure…"

"I'm sure. It's nothing serious. Just something I need to handle. If it's okay, I'd like to go on Wednesday, tomorrow. I have two days off in a row. I would be gone overnight." She winced. She was asking a lot.

"No problem."

She heard the unspoken questions in his voice but chose to ignore them. "And do you have a GPS I can borrow. Getting lost is how I ended up here in the first place."

"There's one in the car. We can't have you getting lost again. Although, I'm glad you ended up on my doorstep." He winked and squeezed her hand gently. "Well, not quite on my doorstep. More in my neck of the woods. If you think about it, I rescued you when I pulled your car out of the ditch. Does that make me your knight in shining armor?"

"No." She drew the denial into three syllables. "Because that would make me a damsel in distress, and that's not a role I want to play." A little thrill ran through her. It would be nice to have someone watching out for her, taking care of her. Though, she didn't relish the idea of someone controlling her again. But a protector would be…acceptable.

"Everyone needs a helping hand now and then. I'd still be wandering if Paul hadn't given me a job and eventually sold me the garage. He helped me find the peace my life was missing."

She liked the way Clint dropped little bits of his history into their conversations. It helped her get to know him. He was an open book, and unlike her, he seemed to have no secrets.

"Technically, he doesn't work here, but yes, that Paul. He just hangs out and putters with cars. He refuses to be paid but doesn't want to get bored. He claims working keeps him young. Who am I to argue with that logic? He's as vigorous now as he was when I first met him."

"I watched him moving cases of oil the other day. He sure isn't weak. He's always pleasant and helpful. I like him. Mathew likes him, too. Calls him Papa for some reason." Initially, her son's fascination with Clint and Paul worried her. But now, Natalie was less concerned. Mathew had stopped asking about Stanley, and that was a good thing. A twinge of guilt pinged that he might forget him, but in the long run, it was probably a good thing. Stanley had never been particularly concerned with Mathew, except that he must go to the best schools and be trained to take over the Walker Empire when he was old enough.

Just that thought made her grind her teeth. She didn't want Mathew growing up in her abusive husband's shadow, which brought her back to her mission for tomorrow.

"So, you're okay if I borrow the car?"

"I am. Are you sure you don't want me to come with you? I could buy you dinner." His words seemed to hint at something more, but she didn't want, didn't need a relationship with him. She refused to admit, even to herself, that she wanted more than friendship from him. An image of his soft touch and the evening of their date flooded her mind. The light touch of his fingers on her arms, the way they'd tugged teasingly at her hair.

No. Stop. Don't go there, don't let yourself want him, don't get attached to him.

The respite she'd found here, in Haven, with Clint, was temporary. She'd have to move on soon and didn't want relationship complications holding her back. The fact she was married only added to the potential complications.

She considered his offer. While the companionship would be nice, she wanted to do this alone. She had to build her independence and learn to rely on herself more. It was nice to have people to do your dirty work for you, but she didn't want Mathew growing up to a life of excess. Now that she'd had a taste of self-sufficiency, she wanted Mathew to have self-reliance, too. The best way to do that was to show him. No preaching, no nagging, just teaching by example. Besides, she'd relied on Clint enough already. It was time to step up and take care of herself. She refused to be the woman who cheated, even mentally, even though she wished she was single.

"I appreciate the offer, but I'm a big girl. I can handle this by myself." She smiled to take the sting out of her words. "But if you wanted to keep half an eye on Mathew, I'd appreciate it. I've never left him alone before. Well, not alone, but you know what I mean."

"I'll watch him like he's my own." Clint slung his arm around her shoulders and pulled her to his side.

She stood frozen inside his embrace, half-facing him.

"Go. Do what you need to do, and I'll keep him safe."

Relief flooded through her, happiness close behind. It was nice to know someone was watching out for Mathew, but at the same time, she was using Clint again. She sighed.

"That was a big sigh." He let the statement dangle.

"Yes." She tried to ignore his questioning smile. "I need to stand up for myself, but here I am depending on you again. Why does this have to be so difficult? Why can't I be independent?"

"Honey, nobody gets by without depending on someone else at one point or another. It's just how life works." He reached out and tugged on a stray lock of hair that had escaped her bun. He wound it around his finger. His gaze drifted from her eyes to her lips and back again.

Good lord! He wasn't going to kiss her, was he? She stared at his lips. What would it feel like to kiss him? Good. It would be good. She wanted to taste him. Needed to.

"Don't look at me like that." A half-smile tilted the corners of his mouth.

"Like what?" She couldn't tear her gaze from his lips.

"Like you want me to kiss you." He leaned a fraction of an inch closer. "Because, I want to kiss you until you can't breathe, until you're weak-kneed and cry out my name and beg me for more." His words were a warning, but she felt them deep inside, like a caress.

Her lips parted on a sigh, and he swooped in, his lips brushing against hers briefly, lightly. She gulped for air, wavered on her feet and leaned into him. Her eyes drifted shut.

He cupped her neck, his fingers cool against her overheated skin, and he backed away an inch.

"I won't do it. I won't shame you by kissing you the way I want to. Not here, in public. Though, Lord knows I want to. I want you." His hand slid lightly down her cheek. "No, I need you. In my life, in my bed." He shook his head. "Not here, not now. But mark my words, Natalie. Someday, I'm going to make love to you. The way I want to, the way you deserve."

She risked a glance at him; his eyes were dark with passion, with warning.

"One day, I'll come after you. When you're free of the past, of your husband." He spat out the last word distastefully. "One day, I'll claim the gift you just offered me." He took a large step backward, his fingers trailing across her shoulders and down her arm until he grasped her fingertips lightly. "Go to work." He cleared his throat. "Before I'm tempted to take more than I should." He released her hand slowly.

She choked out some kind of reply then fled from his words, from his passion. From the emotions that threatened to swamp her.

Natalie scurried through the restaurant. Behind her, she heard Lisa and Clint talking. She raced out the door and around the corner, where she collapsed, panting, against the side of the garage.

Holy smokes.

Good grief.

Her heart pounded, her blood rushed through her veins and her cheeks heated.

He'd kissed her. In public.

And she'd liked it. Dear God in heaven, she'd liked it. It had been hardly more than a brush of his lips across hers, but electricity had jumped between them. She was sure anyone watching would have seen the sparks. Oh, Lord. People had seen them!

She was a married woman, for Pete's sake. And she'd kissed another man!

And I liked it, too.

Her fingers traced her lips, mimicking his kiss. She'd felt more from that one brief touch than she'd ever felt from her husband. Her body was on fire. She wanted more. Much more.

Oh, she was in trouble.

Big trouble.

NATALIE PULLED the car onto the highway. The GPS was set for Edmonton. There were a number of small towns closer, but she needed a big city, with pawn shops.

Things were tight. She was out of money, and that left her with only one option. Pawn her jewelry. She had diamond earrings, a diamond pendant, a gold bracelet and her wedding rings. Surely, she'd get enough for them to buy some necessities. Mathew was growing like a weed. He'd outgrown most of the clothing she'd snatched when she'd fled. He was starting to grumble his underwear hurt. He needed something that fit better, and he needed a few new toys. Nothing expensive, nothing fancy. Just basic clothing and toys. Her underwear was in tatters. One would have thought undergarments that cost an arm and a leg like hers would last longer. Apparently not. She needed new ones. She sure didn't want Clint to see the collection of holes that made up her panties.

Whoa, girl! Where had that thought come from? She had no intention of letting Clint see her in any state of undress. Did she?

She tapped her fingers on the steering wheel and sighed. She was in a fine state. Lusting after one man, running from another. Life was too complicated. "I will not sleep with him."

Whether or not she slept with Clint was irrelevant. She still needed new undergarments. No more silk and lace. Plain utilitarian cotton would be cheaper and would suffice. She was making ends meet, sort of, by working at the bookstore. But there was no room in the budget for frivolity. There was barely room for necessities, and that was what had led to the decision to hock her jewelry.

The disobedient part of her mind wondered what it would be like to make love to a generous, giving man like Clint, instead of a jerk like her soon to be ex. But she could never be that woman, a woman who cheated, even if she hated her husband with a passion.

"Get a grip, Walker." She forced herself to stop hyperventilating and take slow, even breaths.

Maybe, Grace was right. Maybe, Natalie needed to become proactive and take the first steps in divorcing Stanley. But a divorce cost money. Lots of money, if she had to fight Stanley every step of the way. She didn't have that kind of cash. Hell, she was barely getting by as it was. And what if he won custody of Mathew? She couldn't live without her son. If Stanley had custody, she'd have to go back to him to keep Mathew safe. It would slowly kill her to be back under Stanley's control. She couldn't live like that again after tasting freedom, limited though her freedom was.

She banged her hands repeatedly against the steering wheel. "Damn, damn, damn." Was there no way out of this besides hiding?

"Come on, girl. You can do this. You can find a way out of this mess. You escaped once. Give yourself time to come up with a new plan. A plan that leads to true freedom and independence." Pushing aside the formulation of plans, she focused on driving to the pawn shops she'd found using the computer at work.

It would take five hours to get there without stops. She'd sell her jewelry as quickly as possible. With luck, she'd make it back tonight, without having to squander money on a hotel room.

She'd budgeted the better part of one day to get the job done, but construction delays and heavy traffic kept her from reaching the pawn shops before they closed. It hadn't occurred to her they might not be open evenings. So, she spent a night in a cheap motel and hit the ground running the next morning. The smaller items were easy to get rid of, but nobody wanted to touch her rings. It seemed shops were wary of rings as expensive as hers, without irrefutable proof she owned them.

Finally, she stumbled upon an independent jewelry store with a sympathetic owner, a man who remembered the rings and Stanley.

"I remember these." The older man smiled.

Natalie's heart stopped in her chest then jerked into overtime. Shit. What were the chances she'd wind up here, trying to sell her rings?

"I commissioned them from my granddaughter, just after she finished learning goldsmithing and started working for me. She has a gift for design. I hated to sell them." He gave her a steely look that chilled Natalie right through. "Why are you selling them? And what proof do you have that they're yours?" He eyed her meager clothing. There were questions in his eyes but no judgment.

Abruptly, she decided to take a chance on a man who professed such adoration for his grandchild. Surely, he had a big heart. "My name is Natalie Walker. My husband is Stanley Walker. I can show you ID. Frankly, I've left my husband. I've run out of money to feed my son, and I can't go back." Her voice cracked with emotion.

"Why not?" He looked at her compassionately.

Natalie worried her bottom lip with her teeth. Finally, she thought, *nothing ventured, nothing gained.* At least, he hadn't already called the police. "He's an abusive son-of-a-bitch. I've had enough of his crap, and I won't let him hurt my son."

"Good for you, Sweetheart." The jeweler's face burst into a full smile. "I hated selling him this set. He's an arrogant SOB." He said with a grimace.

"Why did you sell the rings to him?"

"Honestly, it isn't easy to make a living and survive against all the chain stores and discount houses. My store is small, and at that time, I wasn't well-known. I needed the money. So, I sold this set to him, against my better judgment."

"It's a lovely set. I adore them. I just hate the man they came from. Please, take them back." She'd get down on her knees and beg if it would help.

"I'll take them back, and I'll give you the fifty thousand he paid me because our reputation has grown and I can resell them for more. I'll find them a worthy home." As if he realized what he'd implied, he added, "not that you aren't worthy, but…"

"But my ex was not. I'm not offended."

"I'll go get you a bank draft."

"Um, could I have cash?" Natalie hated to ask, but bank drafts meant banks and questions she wasn't ready to answer.

He seemed startled.

"Look, I can prove who I am. To you. But if I go to a bank, Stanley can trace me, and I'm not ready for that."

"It's difficult to get that kind of cash. It could take a while."

"I'll wait." Relief flooded through her, and she felt herself relax for the first time since leaving Haven. She checked back into the motel and called Clint to let him know she would be delayed. She let Grace know, too, and wouldn't make it to work tomorrow.

It wasn't until the next morning that the jeweler had the cash and Natalie was able to make her way back to Haven. A full fifty hours had passed since she'd left. When she pulled into the garage parking lot, Clint exploded from the building. He was across the lot and had her door yanked open before she'd even come to a complete stop. She barely had time to grab her purse.

"Jesus. I was worried sick. Where the hell were you?" He jerked her from the car and into his arms.

His anger was at odds with his obvious relief at seeing her.

"I called you. I told you I'd be delayed." She didn't understand his intensity. All around the yard, people stared at them. Nobody made any attempt to disguise their interest.

"What's going on?" She gestured at the crowd. "Why is everyone staring?"

"Haven't you been listening to the news?" Clint grabbed her by the arm and towed her toward the building.

"Ow, that hurts." She pulled back on her arm. "Let me go!"

"Not until we get to the bottom of this." He kept pulling, though his grip loosened a bit.

"Stop. Dammit, let go of me. I'm not going with you. I need to see Mathew." Panic laced her voice. "He's okay, isn't he?"

Clint stopped walking, then released her arm. "Mathew's fine. You aren't. Haven't you been listening to the radio?"

"No. I was listening to your CDs. What's on the radio?" She was totally bewildered by the intensity of his distress. Fear raced through her. What was going on? What happened?

"Come inside. Please. You have to see this. Before the police get here." He led her through the restaurant, urging her to go faster with every step. People stared at them, and the shocked whispers began, growing with intensity as more and more people noticed them.

"You're making a scene."

"No, you're making a scene." He dragged her into the office and closed the door behind them. He pushed her gently into his desk chair, fiddled with the computer and a news report started. "Watch."

A perky blonde news anchor gave the camera a concerned look.

"Last night, Vancouver was shocked at the surprise death of business mogul, Stanley Walker."

Natalie gasped.

"The police are asking anyone with information on his wife's whereabouts to come forward. She's wanted for questioning in his suspicious death."

Natalie's picture flashed on the screen as the anchor rattled on, but her words faded under the buzzing in Natalie's ears.

She stared at the screen, unable to comprehend. She sat, not seeing, not hearing, oblivious to everything but the emotions running rampant through her. First shock, then relief, then fear. Sudden blazing, mind-numbing fear. She gasped, and gasped again, her vision blurring.

"Breathe." Clint shook her by the shoulders. "Dammit, Natalie. Breathe."

She forced herself to listen. "Oh my God. You think I did this!" She bolted to her feet. "I didn't. I couldn't." She started hyperventilating again.

"Natalie, stop. You're getting hysterical." When she didn't calm down and kept babbling, he grasped her shoulders and shook her gently. Not hard, just enough to jolt her to reality. "Of course, I don't think you did it."

"Oh God, oh God, oh God." She groaned. "Mathew! I have to get to Mathew. We have to go!"

"You're not going anywhere," a voice at the door stated.

Natalie looked up to see Mac standing there, dressed in his full RCMP uniform. She wobbled on her feet, her knees went weak and everything went black.

When she came to, she was slouched in Clint's chair.

"What hap—" Her memory flooded back. "I didn't…"

"Don't say anything else." Clint clamped his hand over her mouth.

"That's right, ma'am." The officer stepped toward her. "I'm

McKenzie Stewart, RCMP. I'm placing you under arrest for the murder of Stanley Walker." He began reading Natalie her rights.

Disbelieving that things could be this bad, Natalie stared at him until he finished speaking. He stood there, staring at her expectantly.

"Do you understand?"

"Understand what?" she parroted.

"Do you understand your rights as I have read them?"

She hadn't heard a word he'd said, but she nodded in agreement anyway.

"Ma'am, do you understand your rights?" He tapped one foot against the tile.

"Yes." She could barely form the word. Her heart pounded. She was being arrested for a crime she hadn't committed. How the hell would she get out of this? And what about Mathew?

"I have to take you into custody." The officer pulled out his cuffs.

"No, no, no." She tried to get around him and out the door. "Mathew, my son. I need to see my son." The officer was a gigantic man; she couldn't squish past him.

"I'll look after Mathew." Clint gestured for Mac to put away the cuffs, grasped Natalie's hand and stroked her fingers. "Go with Mac. We'll get this straightened out."

"But I didn't do it. I was—"

Clint's finger pressed against her lips. "Shh. I've got Mathew. I know you didn't do it. Go with Mac." He nodded toward the RCMP officer. "Mathew and I will be right behind." He turned toward his friend. "Where are you taking her?"

"Edmonton. Pending charges, she'll be flown to Vancouver for the investigation."

"And her son?"

"Social services will collect him and take him into their care." Mac appeared uncomfortable.

"No." Natalie wobbled on her feet. She flopped back into the chair and sucked in some deep breaths. This wasn't happening. It couldn't be happening.

"Sorry, ma'am. It's procedure."

"I've got this," a feminine voice said. Everyone turned to look at the newcomer.

"Jessie, thank God, you're here. Jessie will help out." Clint waved Jessie into the room.

"What? Why?" Natalie couldn't form a coherent sentence.

"Lisa called me." Jessie, Doc Hardy's nurse, turned toward Mac. "Before you take her away, I have some paperwork regarding temporary custody of Mathew. Can we have a moment?"

"I can't leave her alone."

"Come on, Mac," Clint said. "We've been friends for years. You trust me, right? Don't give me that skeptical look."

"Where's she gonna go?" Jessie asked. "There's no window and no other door. Stand outside. Shut the door. Give us a minute. Please. I'm asking you, as an officer of the court."

Mac scrutinized Jessie, then Clint. Finally, he looked at Natalie. "You'll stay here?"

Natalie nodded.

Mac stepped outside and pulled the door shut. Through the door, they heard him shooing people away. Finally, silence fell.

"Natalie, I've got some paperwork for you." Jessie placed some papers on the desk. "When we first heard the news, we started things rolling."

"I didn't do it!" Natalie's hands shook, and chills chased up and down her back. It hurt to draw a breath. She wanted to crawl into a hole or run screaming from the room.

"We know," Clint and Jessie said in unison.

"This isn't about you," Jessie continued. "This is about Mathew. We need to arrange his custody. Temporary custody. I'm with social services. Haven doesn't need a full-time worker, so I step in on the rare occasion a social worker is needed. I can set it up so Mathew is cared for by someone who loves him while you're gone."

Natalie stared at her blankly, wishing her brain would work, that the buzzing in her ears would stop. "I need a drink." Natalie's mouth felt like cotton. It was so dry she could hardly form words. She couldn't think. She could hardly breathe.

Clint stuck his head out the door and shouted, "I need a glass of water."

Half a minute later, Lisa handed it to him.

"Drink this." He moved around the desk and gave Natalie the glass.

Gratefully, Natalie sucked the water back. The cold rushed to her stomach, unsettling her, and for a moment, she worried the fluid might come back up.

"Who do you want to have temporary custody of Mathew?" Jessie tapped her pen on the papers.

"Oh, God. I don't know. Not Stanley's family."

"I'll take him, Nat."

"You?" Natalie stared at Clint.

"I love him like my own. He likes me." He knelt in front of Natalie. "I'll keep him safe."

Natalie looked him in the eyes. He seemed so sincere. Could she trust him?

"I love him. And I love you."

It was there, in his eyes. The truth. His love shone there for Natalie to see. But she didn't acknowledge it. She couldn't.

"If I give Clint custody, can I change it later?"

"Yes. This is temporary custody. A provision for care in your absence. We can alter it later. This keeps Mathew out of foster care. Do you want Clint to care for him? Don't hesitate to say no." Jessie shot Clint an apologetic look, and he smiled to show her she hadn't hurt his feelings.

"Yes." Natalie wrapped her arms around herself and gave Clint a beseeching look. "Please look after him for me."

Ten minutes later, the forms were filled out, making Clint temporary guardian of Mathew. Tears streaked down Natalie's face. She buried her face in her hands, her shoulders shook with sobs.

Clint drew her into his arms. "Come on, honey. We have to do this. I'll watch Mathew. You have to say goodbye. We'll follow you to Vancouver. I'll bring him to visit you."

"No!" She pushed him away and glared. "He can't see me in prison."

A knock sounded at the door, and it opened a crack. Lisa poked her head inside. "I've brought Mathew."

Mathew stepped inside the room, took one look at his mother and raced into her arms. He patted her gently and touched a tear. "Why are you sad?"

"Mommy is sad because she has to go away for a few days. Mr. Clint will look after you."

"But you were already gone. I misseded you."

"And I missed you." She grabbed a tissue from the box on the desk and wiped her eyes. "It's only for a little while. You get to play with Mr. Clint while I'm gone. He'll take you to a hotel with a pool, and you can swim and go to the zoo or the aquarium." She didn't even glance at Clint for confirmation. She knew, deep inside, he'd do what she wanted.

"You better believe it, Sport. You and I are going to have a great time while your mom is gone. Give her a kiss, and we'll go pack some things for you. Then we'll go for a long drive. Maybe, we can even go fishing."

"I love fishing and da-quarium." Mathew wiggled excitedly. While he had never been fishing, he had a favorite fishing video game. He kissed Natalie, grabbed Clint by the hand and started tugging him toward the door.

"One minute, Sport."

Natalie watched Mathew with Clint. They were good together. She relaxed a bit, knowing Clint would take good care of him. "Thank you." She waved to Clint.

He pulled her into his arms and looked at her. He whispered

quietly, so the others couldn't hear. "You're not a married woman anymore." Slowly, giving her a chance to stop him, he lowered his mouth and kissed her. Softly, then deeply.

Blood pounded in her ears, until the sound softened to a dull roar. Then all thought fled, and she gave herself up to the passion and love in his touch. Gently, he pulled away.

"I love you. Be safe. We'll get you out of this." He didn't wait for her to reply; instead, he took Mathew by the hand and led him away. He turned to Mac as he passed by. "No cuffs. She won't run. Give her some dignity."

Mac nodded. Once they were out of sight, he turned to Natalie. "I'll need to search your purse before we go."

She handed it over without comment.

He rifled through it, removed a nail file and a couple pens then handed it back.

"Shall we go, ma'am?" His tone was casual, as if he were asking her to cross the street.

Unable to stem her tears, Natalie nodded and followed Mac out of the office, grateful the restaurant was almost deserted now. She didn't stop to wonder why the customers had left. She was relieved that only three women remained to watch this embarrassing moment.

Jessie, Grace and Lisa each hugged her at the front entrance. "Take care," they said in unison.

Mac led her outside to an empty parking lot. The only person in sight was the gas station attendant, who was conspicuously occupied, his back toward them.

Mac escorted her into the RCMP cruiser then pulled out of town. No words passed between them. At length, Natalie forced herself to sleep to escape the deafening silence between them.

The trip to Edmonton, the brief interview at the police station, and the subsequent flight to Vancouver were nothing more than a blur to Natalie. She didn't understand why they couldn't complete her questioning in Edmonton. Instead, they shipped her to a remand center in Vancouver.

Natalie hung her head in shame. She hadn't killed Stanley, but nobody believed her. She was strip-searched, given prison garb and placed in a holding cell. Then the battering began. Question after question. She'd seen enough cop shows to know not to answer without a lawyer, so she steadfastly refused to respond to any questions until she hired one.

She was at a loss as to who to hire. She was reluctant to use Stanley's team of lawyers, who'd always struck her as sketchy. Something about the way they did business bothered her. Instead, she called Belinda. She'd been through a long, successful court battle when her father had died without a will.

"Oh my God. I couldn't believe it when I saw the news. I knew you wouldn't do anything like that. You're one of the gentlest people I know." Belinda's words were a balm to Natalie's sagging spirits. Despite them being in town in case she needed something,

Natalie hadn't seen Clint or Mathew. She'd asked them to stay away. No child needed the trauma of seeing his mother in jail.

Natalie sighed. "Thanks for believing in me. They haven't given me long to talk, so I have to get right to the point. I remember the trouble you had when your dad died. Can you call your lawyer for me? See if I can hire him?"

"I'll do that right now. I can't come down because Justin is getting worse, but if you give my lawyer permission, he can keep me updated."

"I'll do that." That was a promise Natalie was willing to make. "Thank you so much for the help. And for believing in me." She hung up the phone, and the guards led her back to her cell. Thank God for old friends who believed in her and were willing to help out.

The next morning, bright and early, Emerson Park arrived.

Dressed in a high-end suit and carrying a designer briefcase, the dark-haired, brown-eyed lawyer was all business.

His first words made her reconsider her decision to hire him. "Don't misunderstand this…but did you murder your husband?"

"Oh my God! No!" Natalie leapt to her feet and stared at him across the table in the interrogation room. How could he accuse her of such a thing? Wasn't he supposed to support her?

"Relax, Mrs. Walker." He gave a wave toward her chair. "I just had to see your reaction. I've learned that surprise often gives me the best judge of guilt or innocence. Your outrage and tears show me you didn't kill your husband."

"Well, thanks for that." She almost felt bad for the sarcasm in her voice. Almost. "Don't lawyers represent guilty people all the time?"

"Some do. Most do." Emerson tapped his chest. "I do not. And it's cost me potential partnerships in several prestigious firms, which is why I've opened my own firm." He gave her a small smile. "Please, Mrs. Walker, sit down, and let's take this from the top."

Natalie eyed him up and down, still angry he'd doubted her.

"Please sit." When she made no move to sit, he continued anyway. "I handle a variety of cases, most of them involving inheritances. I began my career in criminal law and spent seven years defending wrongfully accused people. It's my intention to have you released on bail as quickly as possible and to get this cleared up quickly."

Natalie lowered herself into the chair but didn't fully relax. "I did not kill my husband."

"Why did you leave him?"

She glared at him. She was sick and tired of questions and accusations.

He met her gaze with patience and a slim smile.

"He beat me, and he threatened my son. I was a virtual prisoner in my own home, so when the chance came, I got the hell out of there. Money or no money. Marriage or no marriage. I refused to let him endanger Mathew. The only way to keep us safe was to hide. So, I hid."

"Where?"

"I was headed toward Hinton, to Belinda's ranch. I didn't tell her when I was coming. I didn't want to leave any evidence of where I was going. But I got lost and crashed my car near Haven."

"Haven, Alberta?"

She nodded.

"Is there anyone there who can prove you were there all this time?"

"The tow truck driver who pulled me out of the ravine. My son and I have lived in his trailer the entire time."

"You lived with him? That won't look good," Emerson said, frowning.

"No. I lived in his holiday trailer. He has his own house."

Emerson nodded. "The police tell me you weren't in Haven when your husband was killed. Where were you?"

"Edmonton." Natalie sighed. "I can't prove where I was for every minute, but I can tell you where I stayed and where I pawned my jewelry." Slowly, bit by bit, she explained where she'd been for the past few days, what she was doing and why.

"So, you spent the first night in a motel, pawned some stuff and then a second night while you waited for the money for the rest?"

"Yes. Is that bad?"

He ignored her question. "Did anyone else see you during that time?"

"I bought food and a couple drinks at a convenience store and stayed in my room waiting for the jeweler to call. I called Clint from the hotel."

"The timing doesn't serve you well. It leaves you enough time to drive to Vancouver, kill your husband and get back."

"I didn't kill him." She choked back a scream. "I'm glad he's dead. But. I. Did. Not. Kill. Him." She ground out the words through gritted teeth. "Talk to his freaking PI. I think his name was Perkins. If anyone knows about his enemies, it's that sleaze-ball."

"Relax, Mrs. Walker. I believe you. We just have to find out who did kill him. I'll put an investigator on it right away. If we find this Perkins, we'll question him."

Natalie watched and listened as he made a phone call, telling someone to investigate her husband, his history, his friends and basically anything that might lead to his enemies.

He pocketed his phone.

"Okay, Mrs. Walker. We can't delay the interrogation any longer."

Natalie sighed. She wasn't ready for this. She didn't think she ever would be.

"Okay, but call me Natalie." She detested being called Mrs. Walker.

"Fine. Natalie it is, in private, but when anyone else is around, we'll stick with the formalities. You're Mrs. Walker, and I'm Mr. Park. Professionalism at all times. When the questions start, answer only what they ask. Don't add any details. Keep your answers short and sweet. After they address you, let me decide which ones you should answer before you say anything. They're going to be rough. They'll ask hard questions and try to shake your calm. They'll try to piss you off and make you upset. Don't let them rattle you. Don't let your emotions get the best of you. Take your time to think before you answer, and above all, remain calm. Are you ready?" He stood and moved to the door.

Natalie took several calming breaths. "As ready as I'll ever be."

"Good." He opened the door and invited the police in. "Mrs. Walker is ready to answer your questions."

There were two officers. A short, stocky blond and a tall, thin brunette. Both looked as if they had the power to snap her in half. They flashed their badges and gave their names, but she was too stressed to remember who was who, so she mentally dubbed them Blondie and Skinny. Briefly, she wondered if they would play good-cop bad-cop.

Officer Blondie started with a statement. "Last Thursday night, a woman about your size, wearing a trench coat with a scarf on her head, was seen boarding, then leaving, your husband's yacht."

"My husband has a yacht?" When did he get a yacht?

"Yes, as we're sure you already know," Officer Skinny replied derisively.

"That's news to me." Natalie looked at her lawyer for clarification.

"He purchased it two years ago. Didn't you know?" Emerson looked sympathetic.

"Frankly, I probably wasn't privy to half of what he purchased. He usually just came home with stuff and showed it off. He has more cars than ten people need. He has eight motorcycles he's never driven. But I didn't know he had a boat."

Why the hell hadn't she kept better track of what he was doing? She knew the answer. As long as he wasn't bothering her or criticizing her for some imagined wrong, she was content to let him do whatever the hell he wanted to do.

The four hours that followed were the worst of Natalie's life.

Question after question and accusation after accusation. The police harassed her, doubted her and made her want to scream.

"Why did you kill him?" Skinny asked for the seventh time.

Rage overcame her forced calm, and she leapt to her feet. "I did not fucking kill Stanley! He was a lying, cheating, no good, son-of-a-bitch. And I wanted him dead. I wanted him gone. Out of my life and away from my son, but I did *not* kill him." She pounded her fists on the table. "I hated him with every fiber of my being, but I didn't kill him." She broke down sobbing and flopped into her chair. She bawled into her hands for several minutes, weeping and sobbing until the anger eased. Slowly, she raised her head, pulled a tissue from the box on the table and wiped her face. She blew her nose into a second tissue and forced herself to relax.

"Yes, I hated him, but I would never do anything to separate myself from my son. I would have run and hid for the rest of my life, but I could never take another life. At least we were safe where we were in Haven, but we lived in fear Stanley's goons would track us down. And if they had, I would've run again. But you have to believe me, I didn't kill my husband. Are we done now? Can I go back to my cell?"

"Cheating?" Officer Skinny asked, seeming to believe her.

"I never caught him, but I smelled perfume on him often, and he never accounted for his whereabouts to me."

"And you didn't care?" Blondie asked.

Natalie thought about the agent's comment for a moment. "At first, I did, but Stanley wasn't an ideal husband. I regretted marrying him from the start and wished I could divorce him. But as time went on, I got pregnant, and I was glad he took his 'affections' elsewhere."

"Why didn't you divorce him?" Blondie asked, accusation heavy in his voice.

Laughter flooded through Natalie. Divorce him? As if! When she finally regained control of herself, she said, "are you familiar with my husband?" She looked back and forth between the two officers. "Do you know he's a powerful man with a lot of enemies and even more clout? He's got several judges in his pocket. Do you really think I could win in a divorce case? Who do you think would get custody of Mathew? Seriously? Why didn't I divorce him?" She laughed wryly. "Think about it. It doesn't take a genius to figure that one out." Why was it so hard for the rest of the world to see what was so painfully obvious to her.

To her surprise, both officers nodded.

"Can I please go back to my cell?" Her head pounded, and she was finding it difficult to think. "The stress is getting to me." God, she just wanted to be alone.

The two officers had a private conference in the corner and turned back to her. "You can go back to your cell for now. We'll pick this up tomorrow."

"What about bail? Can I get out of here? I swear, on the life of my son, I won't leave the city."

"That's a matter for a judge. For tonight, you'll remain the guest of the province."

"Funny." There wasn't a trace of humor in her voice. "Very funny."

EVERY MORNING, for the next three days, Skinny and Blondie returned with more of their questions. They covered the same territory over and over again until Natalie was so sick of it she wanted to scream. The only saving grace was that at the end of every interview, Emerson let Natalie use his cell phone to call Mathew.

"Mr. Clint and I wented to da'quarium. We saw lots of fishes and whales and stuff."

Natalie was thrilled Mathew was enjoying himself, but every conversation made her heart break a little more. When would she get out of here? It was killing her to be away from Mathew.

"And Grammy lets me play blocks in the sunroom." He sounded happy and carefree.

"Grammy?" Natalie asked, having no idea who Mathew meant.

"We comed home, and Colleen was here and Grammy, too."

What the hell? Why did Clint take Mathew to their old home? Didn't he realize what awful people they were? She'd told him she didn't want Mathew near them. Panic seized her. What if Clint left Mathew there alone with them? *Don't freak out. Don't scare Mathew.*

"Honey, can I talk to Mr. Clint again?"

"But I didn't tell you about the puppy."

Tears welled at the plaintive tone of his voice.

"You can tell me tomorrow. Why don't you go draw me a picture and let me talk to Mr. Clint. I love you, Mathew. Forever." She waited while he gave the phone to Clint.

"What can I do for you, Natalie?" Clint asked when he finally came on the line.

"You can tell me why the hell you took Mathew back to that place…to those…those people," she demanded.

"Relax, Sweetheart."

"Don't say that. Don't call me Sweetheart. Get him out of there now. Now, Clint." Her voice rose louder with each word.

"Natalie, stop it. Eugenia loves him. She adores Mathew. I'll admit I was reluctant to bring him here. At first. But he was losing it. Bad. He needed a familiar face. He likes me, but I'm not family. So I brought him home. Eugenia would never do anything to hurt him. She deserves to see her grandson. She isn't who you think she is."

"I can't believe you took Mathew to my mother-in-law's. Get him out of there." She was hysterical. She strove for calm. "Clint, I'm begging you. Please, please, get him out of there." Tears rolled down her face.

"He likes it here, Nat. I didn't tell you, but every day he was getting harder to handle. He misses you. Being in a familiar place is helping him stay calm. I haven't left him alone here. I won't leave him alone."

Natalie whimpered into the phone. "Please."

"What if whoever killed Stanley is still out there and wants something we don't know about?" Clint asked calmly. "We need to keep Mathew protected."

"Protected? There?" Chills raced down her back. Oh, God, could her son be in danger? "Everyone there is one of Stanley's goons." Why wasn't Clint getting this?

"Not anymore. Colleen is a wonder with Mathew, and Eugenia adores him. We've fired all of Stanley's men and hired new guards. The only staff left are the maid and Colleen. Everyone here has been vouched for by Mac. He's a cop, for Pete's sake. Natalie, I swear on my life Mathew is safe."

"Clint. Get. Him. Out. Of. There. Now!" She gasped out the words. Her chest was tight, and she was getting lightheaded.

"Natalie, I promise not to let him out of my sight. You trusted me with his care; trust me now. Trust me on this. I have to go. Mathew wants me to meet his new puppy. I love you. See you soon."

The line went dead, and Natalie stared at the phone in disbelief. He'd hung up on her.

"I have to get out of here."

"Mathew is safe."

"You knew about this?" she screeched. Whirling around, she flung the phone at Emerson. It bounced harmlessly off his chest and landed with a thunk on the floor. Panic clawed at her throat, stealing her breath.

"You told me to keep an eye on him. He's safe with his grand-mother. She adores him, and she had nothing to do with Stanley's death. I'm sure of it."

"I want him out of there. Now!" Natalie pleaded.

"I've watched them together. She cried when she saw him. She adores Mathew. She dotes on him. I've never seen anyone so happy to see a child. Frankly, I think she's almost relieved her son is gone."

"I don't care what you think. Get him out of there, and get me out of here."

"I'm doing everything I can to get you out. I have an appointment with the judge this afternoon. With luck, we can have you released tomorrow." He bent and picked up the phone off the floor. He didn't check to see if it was damaged. He just slipped it inside his jacket pocket.

"I swear on my life your son is safe, and we'll get this figured out as quickly as we can. I'll come back as soon as I know something."

~

NATALIE PACED BACK and forth in her cell for hours. She didn't have the stomach to talk to anyone. She hated this place. She didn't belong in a prison. She just wanted to hold Mathew and go back to living a normal life.

She worried, she fretted and she tried to not give in to the panic cresting over her in waves.

Holy hell, what was Clint thinking, taking Mathew back into that viper's den? Didn't he understand how evil it was, how horrible things were? A small voice in the back of her mind told her Eugenia had always been kind to Mathew, had always been gentle with him, but Natalie refused to listen to that voice. She refused to hear anything good about that family.

What the hell had she been thinking to marry Stanley? She'd married him, hoping to please her father. She just wished she'd known at the time she was trading the devil she knew for the one she didn't. She'd traded disappointment for hell-on-earth.

And now, Mathew was living in that hell, and there was nothing she could do about it.

CHAPTER 18

Clint looked at Eugenia. "That didn't go particularly well. She's royally pissed."

"Do you blame her?" Natalie's mother-in-law rolled her chair closer to Clint. "Her life here was a nightmare. My son was a bastard and a mean son-of-a-bitch."

Clint contemplated her, shocked.

She laughed at his surprise. "I was never able to please him. From the day I married Stanley's father, your father, I was under pressure to be perfect." She shook her head sadly. "I should have left him years before he died and before we had children. Lord knows, I was never happy with him. But I was young, so young, and I stayed."

Clint patted her hand reassuringly. "We all make mistakes, but I don't know how I'll ever get Natalie to understand why I brought Mathew home, let alone explain why I didn't tell her who I am."

"It probably isn't much comfort, but I've got your back." Eugenia squeezed his hand. "I'll help you two work this through."

"Grammy, Grammy. Mr. Clint. My puppy just catched the ball. I throwed it, and he bringed it back." Mathew raced into the room, a large, mixed-breed puppy scampering at his heels.

"He caught it and brought it back." Eugenia blended a grammar correction smoothly with enthusiasm. She clapped her hands. "How wonderful."

Mathew climbed carefully into Eugenia's lap, mindful of the levers on her wheelchair. "I love you, Grammy." He kissed her on the cheek.

"Come now, Mathew." Colleen stood in the doorway. "Grammy and Mr. Clint are talking. Let's go find a leash, and I'll teach you how to take your puppy for a walk."

"Thank you, Colleen." Eugenia addressed the nanny. "You're a lifesaver." She smiled kindly. "It means a lot that you were willing to come back after Stanley fired you."

"I'm glad to be back. I adore Mathew." She ruffled his hair. "We'll be in the backyard. Come on, Mathew. Bring… What are you going to call him?" She nodded toward the puppy.

"Hotdog." He dropped to his knees and hugged the dog. "I'm gonna call him Hotdog, 'cause I love hotdogs and I love him."

Everyone laughed, and Colleen led Hotdog and Mathew from the room.

"He had a mistress," Eugenia said out of the blue when Mathew was out of earshot.

"What? Who? Stanley or his father?"

"Well, both." Eugenia laughed sadly. "But I meant Stanley, my son."

"You know this for sure?" Clint asked.

"I do. She was his secretary for a while. Though, I expect he fired her when he dumped her. That's how his father always did it. Stanley picked up a lot of bad habits from him." She sighed. "My husband wasn't a good man, but he was never abusive. My son was both nasty and abusive."

"We need to tell Natalie's lawyer about the affair." Clint pulled out his phone. He didn't bother to tell Eugenia her deceased husband had once beat Clint's mother almost to death. The man was long dead and wouldn't harm anyone else, so there was no sense adding to the burdens she already carried.

CHAPTER 19

Her first court appearance had felt like a train wreck. The judge denied her bail because he'd considered her a flight risk, even though she didn't have access to her husband's bank accounts.

They had petitioned the court a second time for bail. Luck had been with them when the judge they'd seen initially was unavailable. They'd appeared before an alternate who hadn't considered Natalie a flight risk. She wasn't off the hook, but the judge had released her on bail, trusting she wouldn't run. After ten days locked in a cage, Natalie was glad to be free of the prison and had agreed, reluctantly, to return to the home she'd shared with Stanley and to stay there, with her son, until the police finished their investigation.

After talking to the jeweler and confirming she had booked a room at the hotel, the police had finally agreed it would have been difficult for her to leave Edmonton, drive to Vancouver, kill Stanley and be back in Edmonton in the short amount of time between leaving the jewelry store and going back to pick up her money. She wasn't free yet, but the matter appeared hopeful.

Emerson pulled up across from the front door and put the car into park.

"You can do this. Your husband isn't here anymore. He can't hurt you now."

She shivered in revulsion as she stared up at the house she'd lived in for so long. She didn't want to be there. In fact, nothing could make her return to this place, except for Mathew. He was here.

Emerson's words reassured her.

"But we still don't know who killed him." She couldn't shake her fear, and her voice trembled.

Emerson opened his door and climbed out. "What we know is that a woman went to the yacht, then he was found drowned with lacerations and contusions on his head and a lot of alcohol in his system. We don't know what happened, and the police are looking for his last mistress." He said the word apologetically, as if reluctant to bring up the fact Stanley had carried on affairs with several women.

"So, if they aren't certain he was murdered, why was I arrested? Jail is awful. I hated every minute of it. The questions, the stares, the accusations. The shame, the fear. I'll never forget how I felt. Why did I have to go through that?"

"Because you went missing. Dead man, missing wife, question-able circumstances… It all adds up to something not-quite on the level. You heard the judge; he felt that you were a flight risk. It's fortunate that we got a second chance to apply for bail, due to the fact that the police are now interested in his mistress." He shrugged and closed the door. "Come on. Let's go see your son."

With those words ringing in her head, she didn't care, for now, that she'd spent several days in jail. She just wanted to see Mathew, to hold him in her arms and reassure herself he'd come to no harm. She jumped out of the car and raced inside.

She didn't bother removing the utilitarian running shoes she'd purchased in Haven. Instead, she raced through the massive, elaborately decorated foyer and into the living room. The room had been transformed, and she stopped in her tracks.

The heavy, room-darkening drapes were gone. So were the overstuffed, leather furniture and glass and chrome tables. The expensive, imported carpets were gone, replaced with plush fun-fur throw rugs and a throw rug patterned with roads and cars. The center of the room was filled with an oversized plastic play castle with slides and a swing. The floors were littered with toys, books and stuffed animals. The room had been transformed from cold and stifling to a child's dream playroom.

"What the…" She was unable to put her shock into words.

"Mommy!" Mathew's voice jolted her back to reality, seconds before he burst through the castle door and into her arms. "You're back." He climbed up her legs and into her arms, nearly knocking her onto the floor. "I missed you."

"Oh, Mathew." She hugged him close. "I missed you, too."

"Look what Grammy and Mr. Clint did. They made me a playroom." He jumped out of her arms and raced excitedly around the castle, then back to hug her again. "It's my favorite room ever."

"It's wonderful." She let him drag her into the castle, where he started showing off his collection of toy cars. "But don't you already have a playroom?"

"But it's upstairs, and Grammy has trouble wif her chair." He frowned. "Why does she have a chair?"

"Because I'm old and my legs hurt." Eugenia's voice came from outside the castle.

"Grammy." Mathew raced out of the castle.

Natalie winced, knowing her mother-in-law would chastise the boy for shouting.

"Come here, you young whippersnapper, and give your old granny a kiss." Eugenia laughed.

Childish lip smacking had Natalie sticking her head out the castle door in disbelief to find Mathew cuddled up on Eugenia's lap with his arms around her neck.

"Mathew, sweetie, get down off your grandmother. Sorry, Mrs. Walker." She addressed her mother-in-law in the formal manner her husband had always demanded.

"Nonsense. He's fine. And call me Eugenia, or Genie, or Mom or something besides Mrs. Walker. I've always hated that foolish formal nonsense."

Natalie stared at her mother-in-law. She opened her mouth to say something, but strangely, she was at a loss for words.

"Relax, Natalie. I won't bite. I wanted to spend more time with Mathew, and now, with Stanley gone, I can see him as much as I want."

"Grammy letted me pick this room," Mathew said with pride. "'Cause I'm big enough to pick for myself. And I gots a dog. His name is Hotdog. He sleeps with me. But he's at the bet."

"At the bet?"

"He gots to get a needle. I don't like needles," Mathew explained with the certainty of a three-year-old.

Natalie looked to Eugenia for clarification. "He wanted a puppy, so I got him a puppy." She shrugged. "Today, he's getting his vaccinations at the vet."

"A puppy? In this house?" The entire world had gone crazy.

"In this house. In my home, our home. And it is a home now. Not a mausoleum."

Natalie stared at Eugenia, unable to fathom the changes. She was so much more relaxed and seemed…happy.

"Relax, dear. I'm fine. I've stopped taking the tranquilizers I've been taking for too many years. I haven't lost my mind. Yet." She laughed at her own joke. "It's good to have you back." Eugenia rolled her chair closer to the castle and helped Mathew climb down.

Natalie crawled the rest of the way out of the castle and looked at Eugenia.

Eugenia shook her head sadly. "I'm so sorry I didn't help you sooner. I never should have let Stanley marry you. I should have warned you. I should have helped you get away sooner. I'm so, so sorry."

"Helped me get away sooner?" Natalie parroted.

"Yes, dear." She reached out and patted Natalie's hand. "I stopped taking the tranquilizers months before you left. Just after I had the flu. I was sick for so long, and I didn't take them because they made my stomach worse. After a few days, I realized I felt better without them."

"I remember. You were so sick, for weeks."

"And you were so kind and visited me every day. I haven't taken one since then. I just faked it."

"But you were taking one the day you spilled them, and I stole a few." Had she spilled them on purpose?

"No, I pretended to take them. I hoped you'd help pick them up. And when I counted them, I knew you'd taken some. I was so happy when I found out you were gone. Did you use them on Stanley?" She sounded almost hopeful.

Natalie blushed.

"You did." Eugenia clapped her hands excitedly. "Don't look so shocked. I wasn't always a stodgy, old bird."

Natalie laughed. "But I used them on your son."

"You used them to free yourself from his abuse. Did you think I didn't see it?" she asked.

"I just assumed you didn't care." Natalie winced at her own words.

"When I was stoned, I didn't care, but when I sobered up, I was mortified. I hated Stanley for what he did to you and me." She hung her head. "Can you ever forgive me for not helping sooner?"

Natalie knelt in front of Eugenia. "Mrs. Walker, Genie, I don't blame you. Without those pills, I never would have gotten away." She hugged her mother-in-law tightly. "Thank you for that."

Genie hugged her back, and for a moment, they stayed like that, each wrapped in their own mixture of sorrow, happiness and newfound friendship.

"Why are you crying, Mommy? Grammy?" Mathew asked in a small, worried voice. "Are you sad?"

"We're not sad," Natalie tried to explain. "We're happy. We missed each other, and we're thrilled to be back together." It wasn't exactly the truth, but there was no way a three-year-old would understand the complexities of what had gone on.

"Will Daddy be sad when he comes back?" Mathew looked back and forth between them in confusion, his young mind trying to puzzle out what was going on.

"Oh, sweetheart." Natalie drew Mathew into her embrace. "Daddy's in heaven with the angels. He won't be coming home. He's gone now." Natalie closed her eyes and cuddled Mathew.

He was young enough that the memories of his father would eventually fade to nothing, and that was good. He'd only seen his father in a rage a few times, but that was a memory no child needed to live with.

For all that Natalie despised her deceased husband, she didn't want Mathew having to live with ugly memories. For now, she'd paint Stanley in a good light, and in time, Mathew would be old enough to ask questions and she'd answer them honestly.

"Thank you," Genie whispered when Mathew returned to his play. "You didn't have to do that. You didn't have to hide the truth."

"Yes, I did. Stanley wasn't a good man, but Mathew isn't old enough to understand. It's better if he keeps his few good memories and forgets the bad. Someday, he'll learn the truth."

Genie nodded. "Thank you. I'll leave you to enjoy Mathew. I've been hogging him for too long. You need time with him. I'll see you at dinner." As she rolled away, she called back over her shoulder. "We eat at six, in the kitchen. Don't bother dressing up. It'll be informal, and Mathew will eat with us, like he should."

Natalie stared at her mother-in-law's retreating form. "Wow, things sure have changed around here." She shook her head in bewilderment. "I can't believe this is the same house I left a few months ago.

Once Eugenia was gone, Natalie realized Emerson was still in the room, standing quietly just inside the door.

"Sorry. I forgot you were here." She felt bad for ignoring him.

"You were kind of distracted, but I didn't want to leave without saying goodbye. I'll be in touch every morning to update you. I expect the police will find the guilty party before long. I'll contact an estate judge and see about freeing up the bank accounts so you have money to live on, but it's going to take some time."

"Soon would be good. Bail used up the money I received after selling my jewelry in Edmonton."

"I'll do my best. After all, I want to get paid." He gave her a big wink, saluted her, then disappeared out the door.

Belinda had been right. Emerson Park was a good man to have on your side, and if it took her the rest of her life to repay him for all he'd done, his help would still be worth every hard-earned penny. She was still sitting there, on the floor, listening to Mathew playing happily with his toys, when Clint strode into the room.

CHAPTER 20

"Natalie. You're back." Clint rushed across the room, and before Natalie knew what he intended, he yanked her to her feet and tugged her into his arms for a bone squeezing hug. "Oh my God, I've missed you so badly." He kissed her cheeks then crushed her mouth under his.

She pushed him away from her. "What are you doing? Don't touch me." She took three steps backward.

"I missed you. Didn't you miss me?" He looked crestfallen.

"Yes. No. Never mind. I told you not to bring Mathew here." She shook her finger in his face. "But you did. You didn't listen to me. I told you to keep him safe."

"He was safe here. He is safe here."

"You didn't know that!" Natalie dropped her voice to a whisper. She didn't want Mathew to overhear their argument. He'd been through enough already. "You knew I didn't want him here. Why would you bring him here?" She quivered with an unchecked emotion.

"I didn't bring him here right away."

"But you did and against my wishes." Uncertainty battered her.

She stood motionless, her teeth grinding together. "I thought I could trust you."

"You can trust me." Clint reached out to caress her, and she reared back. His hand dropped limply to his side. "Let me explain."

He didn't give her a chance to object. He just started talking. "After a couple days, Mathew was getting more and more upset. It was breaking my heart to watch him missing you."

Clint's voice was heavy with emotion, and Natalie found herself listening, despite herself.

"He kept asking about you and about his dad. When he started asking about Colleen and Grammy, I knew I had no choice but to bring him here against your wishes. The tension, the uncertainty was getting to him. Mathew's still a baby." He kept his eyes on Natalie as he paced the room. "He's too young to understand. He likes me, but I'm new to him. He needed familiar faces and a place he knew. Before we came back, I replaced all of Stanley's goons with men I trust with my life, and I brought Mathew home."

"I told you not to." She didn't want to understand Clint's reasoning.

"He needed familiar surroundings. I stayed with him. I slept in his room with him. I was here all the time. I was in the kitchen when you arrived. He was—is—happier here." Clint gestured vaguely around to indicate the entire mansion.

Mathew did seem happy at home. Natalie was shocked the unhappy place where she'd spent her entire married life was so different from when she'd left. But she was still angry Clint deliberately disobeyed her.

"He is happy here. But I told you—"

Clint held up a hand to halt her words. "You've said that. Again and again. You weren't here. You don't know what we went through. I knew Stanley was a jerk, but I also knew Eugenia had a good heart and would take Mathew back in and care for him."

"What?" Natalie gaped at him. Her mouth opened, closed then opened again, but she couldn't find the words to express her confusion. Her arms wrapped around her middle, and her hands clenched into tight fists, her nails digging deep into her palms.

"I know you're mad at me." His Adam's apple bobbed as he swallowed. "And this is going to make it worse."

"How can it get worse?" Natalie glowered at him. Frustration spiked up and down her spine. She could tell she wouldn't like what he had to say. She took a deep breath and unclenched her hands.

"I knew Eugenia and Stanley long before I ever met you."

"What the hell?" Natalie blurted, forgetting Mathew was in the room.

"I didn't know who you were, when you first came to Haven, but some of the things you said made me think, and I looked at the registration in your car." He winced as if knowing how bad his poorly worded explanation sounded.

"You snooped on me? You snuck around behind my back?" With each word her voice rose. She was losing control and knew it, but for the life of her, she couldn't calm down. "You knew who I was? You knew Stanley?"

"I snooped, and I kept it a secret. You didn't want to tell me, and I pretended I didn't know, but—"

"But?" Natalie's blood boiled, her heart pounded, and she battled the urge to bolt from the room because she couldn't leave her son here with this…this liar. "There is no 'but'. Jesus, Clint, you should have told me. No," she corrected herself. "You shouldn't have snooped around behind my back."

Clint hung his head.

Natalie looked at him, standing there, looking sheepish. "What? What are you hiding now?"

Was there no end to his lies? Anger filled her. What had he done now? Could this get any worse? She'd thought she loved him, but they'd lied to each other and that was no basis for a relationship. She wanted to curl up in a ball and weep at the unfairness. He was a liar. He was no better than Stanley.

Even as the thought formed, she had to reject it. He was a liar, but not once had he ever hit her or threatened her. He'd shown her nothing but kindness.

"What other lies have you told me?" she demanded.

"Just one," Clint said sadly. "Stanley was my half-brother."

Disbelief rocked Natalie. Her blood roared, and her vision went blurry. "What?" Her voice was shrill, and she didn't care.

"Stanley's father slept with my mother. They had an affair. She thought they were in love, but he lied to her then dumped her when he learned she was pregnant with me. I didn't know about my father. I thought he was dead until Mom passed away and I found a letter she had left me in her things."

She had only the vaguest recollection of him mentioning this, but right now, the details escaped her. She didn't want excuses or a history lesson, she wanted him to shut up, to stop talking, but he rattled on.

"I knew nothing about him or his family until then. When I learned who he was, I came to see him. I hated him from the moment I met him. He was a nasty man. Grasping, greedy and mean. And his son, your husband, was no better. Even Stanley's sisters were greedy and money-hungry. I've never met such a sorry, selfish bunch of people in my life. Except Eugenia. She welcomed me into her home and made my father welcome me, too. She was kind and gracious to me, the bastard son of her cheating husband. She didn't have to be. She could have been as cruel and useless as he was. But she wasn't. Eugenia has always been kind and treated me with respect. That's how I knew Mathew would be safe and welcomed here. I knew Eugenia would welcome us both home."

Natalie stared at him. Jesus, he was Stanley's half-brother. Why hadn't he told her? There were times when she'd suspected he wasn't telling her everything. But not for one moment had she thought he was hiding his past. Why had he kept it a secret? Disappointment rocked her. She knew he had secrets, but not for one moment did she think he was related to her husband. He should have told her.

He reached toward her, and she jerked backward until she pressed against Mathew's castle and she couldn't go any farther without bolting.

"Please leave!" She pointed toward the door. Disillusionment and confusion made her arm tremble, but she ignored it. "I need time to think this over. Don't visit; don't call."

"Natalie." He took a small step toward her. "Let me explain."

"Out." She inched sideways, increasing the distance between them.

"But we don't know who killed Stanley or what they were after. You might not be safe."

"I don't care. Go. Take your hired goons and go." Her voice rang with anger and recrimination. She shook like a leaf. A hurricane of emotion battered her heart. She could barely stand. She wanted to weep, but she refused to give him the satisfaction of seeing her tears.

"I'll go, but I'm leaving my men to guard you."

"Take your goons. We have a state-of-the-art alarm system. I don't need your spies. Get out!" She backed farther away and pointed at the door.

Clint dug his cell phone from his pocket and hit a number. "Pull the men out." He listened to the person on the other end, and a moment later, he added, "I said pull them out." He slid the phone back inside his pocket and stepped toward her.

She tried to back up but bumped into the wall. She had nowhere to go. He moved slowly, until one finger brushed lightly across her cheek, capturing a tear that had escaped, despite her attempts to keep from crying.

"I'm so sorry," he whispered. "I should have told you who I was when I realized who you were, but this family wasn't part of my life any longer. I despised who they were, what they were. I hated their useless, self-centered lives. So I walked away. But I should have told you as soon as I suspected a connection."

She shook her head, denying his apology, refusing to listen.

He caressed her cheek softly and whispered, "I love you, Natalie. If you believe nothing else I've said, believe that. I've loved you since the moment I found you in that ravine."

She closed her eyes, as if closing her eyes to the sight of him could block his words, and keep her from hearing his declarations.

"I love you, Natalie." His hand dropped away from her face, and he slowly walked away. She didn't open her eyes until the room was silent, except for the small sounds of Mathew.

"Why are you crying?" her son asked quietly. "Where did Mr. Clint go? He said we'd play Legos."

"Mr.…Mr. Clint had to go. He'll come play Legos another day." She hated herself even as she said the words. She was no better than anyone else, considering she'd just lied to her son. Though it was to save him from hurt, she'd lied and her heart curled up into a little ball and a part of her died.

"Mommy is tired, Mathew. I'm going to sit and rest for a minute. Then we can play."

Mathew nodded and crawled back inside the castle, and Natalie staggered to the only adult-sized chair left in what had been a formal living room.

She closed her eyes and pressed her hands over her ears, trying to block out the memory of Clint's confession. She trembled with rage, grief and sadness. Her life had gone from bad, to worse, to disastrous.

A soft female voice broke into her thoughts and she opened her eyes.

"Sorry to bother you, Mrs. Walker," Annabelle, Stanley's maid, said quietly. "I'm sorry that Mr. Walker died."

To Natalie's eyes, the maid didn't seem upset. "Thank you." What did Annabelle really want?

"I'd be happy to stay on if I'm welcome. I adore Mathew and Miss Genie. And I've always liked you. You treated me nicely." A light red blush suffused her face, and she looked at the floor.

"And my husband?" Natalie couldn't keep the bitterness from her voice.

"Sorry, Mrs. Walker, I never much cared for your husband, but I do need this job." She shrugged as if to say nothing ventured, nothing gained.

After a moment's hesitation, Natalie said, "call me Natalie. I'm not sure how things will work out. I'm still under suspicion of murder, and I don't know how that will impact Stanley's will or even what his will says." She sighed heavily.

"I understand, Miss Natalie." The gray-haired maid smiled. "I know you didn't do it. We all do. It's only a matter of time until the police find the person who killed him."

"Thanks for the vote of confidence." Natalie was surprised to find she meant it. It was nice to know someone believed in her innocence. "I can't guarantee anything, not even a paycheck, but you're welcome to stay on. If you want to."

"Thank you." The maid grimaced. "I have to tell you something first. I can't work here with this nagging at me."

Oh great. What now? She didn't say anything; she just nodded for Annabelle to continue.

"The day you left, I found Mr. Walker unconscious in the kitchen. And I found a pill on the floor. It looked like one of the tranquilizers I helped Mrs. Walker take." Her gaze darted around the room, and she wouldn't meet Natalie's eyes.

"And?"

"And I didn't wake him up. I left him lying there until he came to on his own. And when he told me to call the doctor and his investigator to find you, I waited. I waited a long time before I called them."

"Why would you do that?" Natalie didn't quite understand the gist of the confession.

"Because I hated him," Annabelle blurted. "For what he did to you, for his mean ways, and I wanted to let you get as far away as possible."

Natalie stared at her, shocked, surprised and strangely thrilled. "I had no idea I had so many friends in this house." She burst into laughter. "I was so wrapped up in my own misery, I completely missed the friends around me." She shook her head at the irony. "Annabelle, I'm sorry I missed your kindness, and I'd be happy to have you stay on. And hopefully, someday, I'll be able to repay you for all you've done for me. And if the estate ever gets settled, I'm giving you a raise." She stood and hugged the maid. "Thank you for being there for me, even if I didn't know it."

"Miss Natalie, you were always nice to the staff. Me and the others. It helped us stay on when your husband was nasty." She smiled warmly and hugged Natalie back. "But that's not why I came in here. Colleen had to run to town, and I thought maybe you could use a break. May I take Mathew to play outside in the sandbox?"

"We have a sandbox?" Natalie blurted.

"Yes, ma'am. Miss Eugenia had it put in while you were…" She shrugged. "She changed lots of things. It sure is different around here. Good different."

Natalie couldn't help but smile at that. "Well, if I don't end up in jail again, a lot of things are going to change around here. By all means, take Mathew outside. As pathetic as it sounds, I could use a break, even though I just got here. Don't forget to take a hat and sunscreen."

"Come on, young Mathew. Let's go play in the sandbox." She smiled broadly when he scurried out of the castle. "Kiss your momma goodnight. She's going for a nap."

"A nap?" he asked in confusion. "But I only just had breffust."

"Mommy's tired. I'll see you after I rest for a bit."

"You're not going away again?" he pleaded.

"I'm staying right here."

"Promise?" he asked, fixing her with a hard stare. If she hadn't been so exhausted, she might have laughed at his fierce expression.

"I promise. I'll nap in your bed, so you'll know where to find me." She hugged him tight and kissed his forehead.

AN HOUR LATER, she sat in the rocking chair in Mathew's bedroom, trying to make sense of the last few months. It felt like years ago she'd drugged Stanley and run away. She smiled a bit at the irony of running away from home at her age.

Her life was such a jumble of messes. Her childhood had been unhappy. She didn't remember her mother, and she'd never been able to live up to the expectations of her father, who'd been a controlling, unhappy man who had all but forced her into a miserable marriage to an abusive man.

Like her father, Stanley had been impossible to please. Nothing had ever been good enough. She'd never been sophisticated, gentle, polite or refined enough to suit him, and she'd paid for her transgressions, real and imagined, in pain and bruises. Unwilling to put Mathew in harm's way, she'd bolted and ended up in Haven.

She smiled at the memory of Haven. A small town filled with the kindest, most caring people she'd ever known. They'd given her a hand when she'd needed it, without making her feel inadequate. She'd matured there and learned to take care of herself. There was such satisfaction in working and being independent from the whims of others.

And I loved Clint, too.

"I thought I loved him, but he was just another liar. I wasn't perfect, I lied to protect myself, but he should have told me who he was." Why had she fallen for his lies? For the life of her, she couldn't figure that out.

Sure, he'd been kind and helpful. Mathew adored him. He'd helped her find a home and helped her get back on her feet without damaging her dignity. He'd treated her with nothing but kindness, but behind it all…lies. Nothing but lies, and she could never forgive him for that.

Now, if only she could erase the image of his smile and his laughing, hazel eyes from her memory. She refused to even think about his touch, the warmth of his arms around her, the laughs they shared or the feel of his lips on hers.

Don't go there, Nat. Nothing good can come from that kind of thinking.

But the thoughts kept intruding, kept pushing their way to the forefront of her mind. She missed Clint and wished that somehow she was wrong about him.

～

"WHAT'S UP, BOSS," Lisa asked Clint when she arrived at work a few days later. "How's Nat? And Mathew?"

"Fine." He frowned.

"Why are you back?" she asked in her typical, forthright manner. "Paul's got things handled here. He used to own the place, you know." She flashed a sarcastic grin.

"I know that." He glared at Lisa when she stepped fully into the office and pulled the door shut behind her.

"What gives?" She put her hands on her hips.

"Out or you're fired." He wasn't in the mood for chitchat with nosy employees.

"She knows, doesn't she?" Lisa flopped into a chair. "I told you to tell her the truth upfront." She shook her head and made a tsking sound. "Man, men are stupid." She drawled the last word into three syllables. "Did she kick ya to the curb?"

"Yes." Clint wasn't at all amused by Lisa's I-told-you-so attitude.

"And you left, just like that?"

"Not just like that. I left guards watching the house. The police don't know who killed her husband yet. I'm playing it safe."

"More like you're keeping your heart safe." Lisa taunted. "You do realize it's too late for that. She reeled you in, hook, line and sinker. And she didn't even have to try. Does she know how much you love her?"

"I told her." God, he hated feeling like this. So helpless, so alone and so angry at Natalie for not listening.

"Does she know you left guards?"

"No."

Lisa doubled over, laughing until she was breathless. "You don't learn, do you?" She tapped her fingers on the desk. "Natalie despises liars. Man, you've got to come clean, because if she ever forgives you for not telling her who you are, this will just flip her over the edge again. Hell, I'd kill ya."

Clint stared at Lisa. Why did she have to be right so often? It was annoying. He sighed. "You're right. How did you get to be so wise?"

"I loved hard, lost early and made a bucketful of mistakes in between." She waved at the phone. "Call her, and tell her. Email her. Text her. Or better yet, talk to her in person. Tell her about the guards. Tell her what you feel. It might come to nothing, but you'll know you've done everything you can to keep her. Don't live your life with regrets. Go after her, boss man." She rose from her chair, crossed the office and kissed him on the cheek. "Don't be a fool, Clint. She's worth the fight."

~

Two hours later, Clint sat on his deck with his longtime friend, Mac, chugging back beers.

"I'm going to go after her." Clint's words slurred a bit due to the alcohol.

"What if she did it?" Mac asked.

"I don't care."

Mac gave him a puzzled look. "You don't care if the woman you love is a murderer? Are you insane? I can tell you, shit like this doesn't end well."

"Frankly, I don't give a fuck. I saw the bruises she had when she got here, and the fear, the deer-in-the-headlights panic. If he beat her, he deserved to die. But I don't think she did it."

"And you know this how?" Mac drawled. "From your years of investigative work?"

"From my years of working with people. Mac, I've known a lot of people. Good and bad. Honest and dishonest. I knew she was hiding something from me. She hid her identity. For good reason. But I know, beyond a shadow of a freaking doubt, she didn't kill anyone. She doesn't have a vicious bone in her body. And she would never jeopardize her custody of Mathew. So, if she says she was in Edmonton hawking her rings, that's where she was. There's no doubt in my mind."

"I wish I had your confidence. I've never met a woman I trusted like that." Mac sighed. "I wish I had."

"It's not just trust." Clint struggled to find the right words. He took a long, deep swallow of his beer. "It's love. There's something about her that calls to me. I need her."

"I need a woman, too," Mac leered, leaving no doubt that he meant sexually.

"Not that way." Clint laughed. "Okay, that way, too. But in my life, forever and ever. Until death do us part and all that stuff. The scary thing is she completes me. I've never felt like this before."

"Did you tell her that?" Mac asked softly.

"I tried." Clint bolted to his feet. "I'll tell her now." He stumbled a few steps forward, and Mac snatched his arm and pushed him back into his chair.

"Sit the fuck down, man. You can go later. When you sober up. You're in no shape to drive, my friend."

"Always the cop." Clint relaxed into the chair.

"Always." Mac agreed. "You can go tomorrow."

~

NATALIE HUGGED Belinda warmly then ushered her inside the house, out of the sun. "I'm so glad you're here." Nat worried that her friend might have overdone it. "Let's go sit in the den. It's cooler in there. Was the drive okay?"

"It was good." They walked through the house. "Well good-ish. I took two days. I stayed in Edson last night."

"Your heart has to be breaking. I am so sorry about Justin. Is there anything I can do?" Natalie patted her shoulder compassionately.

"I can't stop crying." Belinda sniffed. "It's hard."

"Oh, God, I can't imagine losing the man you love." *Liar. What about Clint?*

"Have you seen him yet?" Belinda asked.

"Who?" Natalie pretended she didn't know who her friend meant.

"You're such a rotten liar." Belinda laughed. "You always were. Clint, that's who. We talked a few times when you were in Haven. I could hear the wistfulness in your voice. You were falling for him."

"I was a married woman. I wasn't falling for anyone." She hated the way Belinda could almost read her mind.

"Natalie, I'm not stupid. You never loved Stanley. You married him to please your idiot father, and we both know how well that worked out. Stanley Walker was an asshole extraordinaire. I suspected that long before you told me. The tone of your emails warned me. Girl, we've lived in each other's pockets for too long to keep secrets from each other."

Natalie didn't say anything.

"So, tell me more about this mystery man. Is he handsome? Rich? A real stud muffin?"

Natalie snickered. "Stud muffin? You always did have a way with words.

"Did you take a ride on his love tool? Hubba-hubba."

They laughed together for a moment.

"I didn't. It's not in me to cheat. We hugged a couple times, kissed a couple times. We never even made it to heavy petting. He was just so good to me, so kind. He helped me out without asking for anything."

"So, where is this wonder now?"

"I have no idea. Back in Haven, I guess." She flopped into an armchair.

"What the hell? You don't know? Holy crap, Natalie. I thought you loved him. I would have bet my life on it." Belinda stared at Natalie, refusing to let her look away.

"I thought I did, too, and for a while, when I was in jail…" She rolled her eyes. "I thought we might see each other again. Seriously."

"And he just fucked off?" Belinda sat across from Natalie.

"No, I kicked him out. He's a liar, just like all men." Her fingers tapped restlessly on the chair.

"Get out. From our talks when you were in Haven, I assumed he was perfect for you. At least, that was the impression I got. What was so brutal that you kicked him out?"

"He snuck around behind my back and found out who I was. Then he lied. He never told me he was Stanley's half-brother."

Belinda gaped at Natalie. "His half-brother?" she whispered.

Natalie nodded.

"I didn't get the impression he was one of the useless, idle-rich like Stanley. No offense."

"He isn't. He owns a garage, a café and a campground. He didn't know about his real father until a few years ago. He said he didn't like him. He hated his family's wasteful ways and self-centeredness. After he met them, he didn't have anything to do with them."

"He doesn't sound like such a bad guy. He helped you a lot in Haven."

"He's not a bad guy." Natalie stared at the floor. "But he lied about who he was. I can't abide a liar." Why didn't people understand Clint's lies made him no better than her lying, cheating husband?

"You lied about who you were."

"To protect Mathew. It's not the same thing."

"Did you stop to think he might have been worried you'd lump him in with his useless family? Because, frankly, the Walker clan isn't the greatest bloodline to be associated with."

"Bloodline?" Nat laughed. "They aren't horses."

"I know. Hazard of being married to a rancher for so long." She sobered. "God, I miss Justin. It was so hard to watch him waste away like that. I'm just glad He didn't suffer too long. I loved him since I first met him when I was eight." She sighed, and a few tears slid from her brimming eyes.

She took a moment to compose herself then gave Natalie a hard look. "Take my word for it, couples fight. Love is hard but losing it is harder. I can see it in your eyes. You're torn. You love him. You're just pissed off he lied. Find out why. If Clint is half the man you say he is, he's worth fighting for."

"It's not that easy." Natalie refused to accept her friend's assessment.

"You're making this difficult. Think about it. Think long and hard before you throw away what he has to offer." She sniffed and bit back a few tears. "God, there were days when Justin and I fought like cats and dogs. Over stupid shit. Now, I'd give anything to have him back to fight with. Take my advice, and think it over. Balance the good with the bad, and for God's sake, listen to your heart."

Belinda stood and hugged Natalie tightly. "I'm going to lie down for a bit, I'm still overtired from the long hours nursing Justin. Don't throw away love because of hurt pride."

Seeing the hurt in Belinda's eyes and hearing the pain in her voice, Natalie's heart gave a lurch. Was her friend right? Could

Clint be worth a chance, despite lying to her? Like a freeze-frame movie, images of Clint scrolled through her mind.

Clint kneeling in the mud and muck, trying to make Mathew feel comfortable with him so Clint could help them up the hill after the car crash.

His anger at the bruises on Natalie's arms. The soft tone of his voice when he'd reassured her she was safe from harm.

His kind mannerisms when letting Mathew help with chores with the unhelpful-assistance that three-year-old children give.

The way he'd helped her get back on her feet, to find her inner strength, without once making her feel inadequate or like a charity case. The way he'd helped her shed her useless, idle-rich lifestyle and stand up for herself.

But mostly, the soft, warm light in his eyes when he'd kissed her and declared his love, and the way her heart had leapt in response.

God, she'd fallen for him. Not quite at first sight, not instantaneously, but a little bit at a time. He'd slowly scaled the wall around her heart and filled her darkness with light and love.

Belinda was right. Natalie owed him the chance to explain his lies. Maybe, his reasons wouldn't be enough. Maybe, his reasons were foolish or selfish, but dammit all, she intended to give him the chance to explain himself. Because, if he did love her the way she loved him, he was worth taking a risk on. She'd been hurt before, that was true, but she was learning life and love were never easy.

It was Clint who'd taught her, without words, that when life knocked you down, you got back up again and carried on. Maybe, just maybe, they could find the middle ground and make this relationship work. If not, she'd let it go, but first she had to give him a chance to explain before they spent any more time apart.

She picked up the phone and asked her lawyer if it was okay to return to Haven for a short time. He checked with the judge and called her back with permission to go as long as she reported where she went.

She'd called in a favor from Stanley's second-in-command at

Walker Enterprises. Thankfully, she'd always had a semi-decent relationship with him, and he'd allowed her some money and the use of the chopper for this venture.

She explained to Mathew she had to go visit Mr. Clint for a while. She would only be gone a few hours. She hoped.

CHAPTER 21

Clint had trouble focusing on the figures in front of him. He needed to get this tax paperwork finished and submit his payment so he'd be free to go confront Natalie. She wasn't getting off scot-free. She had to face him one more time before he let her kick him out of her life. But something outside was thumping. A deep, throbbing noise reverberated through the walls of Clint's office, driving him nuts. How the hell was he supposed to concentrate with all that racket?

Irritated, he jumped from his chair and strode through the café and outside to put a halt to the noise. The closer he got to the door, the louder the noise. He could barely push open the door against the thundering wind pressure. When he managed to struggle outside, he stopped dead.

A helicopter?

In Haven?

In his parking lot?

What the hell?

As the blades slowed, the corporate logo on the door became clear. Walker Enterprises.

The door edged open, and a pair of sandaled feet slipped out, followed by long toned legs, a knee-length skirt and the most lusciously curved body he'd ever seen. His heart exploded in double-time beating. It couldn't be… But it was.

Holy Christmas.

Natalie was here.

Good God, don't let anything be wrong, he prayed and bolted toward her.

~

"Please wait for me. I won't be long." Natalie slid down from the helicopter, ducked low and scurried toward the café.

Her hair flew crazily about her face, buffeted by the rotors' backwind. She prayed Clint was inside. She didn't want to waste time looking for him.

She pushed aside her hair to find Clint racing toward her. He had the strangest look on his face, half-smile, half-panic, and she realized she had to do this her way. She held up one hand in a stop motion.

Clint halted where he was, and she moved toward him. Without saying a word, she pointed toward the side of the café, where a few picnic tables sat in the shade. She followed him to the tables and indicated he should sit. Behind her, the helicopter blades slowed and finally came to a stop. When they were silent and the wind gone, she sat across from him.

"Don't say anything." She gave him a pleading look. "I need to say some things. Then you can talk."

"Nat—"

"Clint, shut up."

He looked shocked at her rudeness but closed his mouth and nodded.

"Thank you." She couldn't stop a small grin.

For several, long minutes, she looked around, avoiding his gaze, unable to find the words she'd so carefully rehearsed on her long trip. This wouldn't be easy, but she hadn't counted on it being this hard. Her heart did a rapid little tip-tap, and she closed her eyes, praying for strength.

Clint shifted restlessly on the bench across from her.

Slowly, she opened her eyes.

"I think…" She almost choked on the words. "I think I might have been hasty in throwing you out of my house."

The relief in his eyes made her heart clench, in a good way.

"My life hasn't been easy. Sure, I had everything money could buy—except true friends and love. Nobody survives without those. My father was…" She groped for the right words. "He was a perfectionist, and I never lived up to his standards. Nothing I did was ever good enough. I was too klutzy, too fat, too bold, too loud. Or I was too quiet at a charity function, never reaching out to take money from charity supporters. Nothing I did was right. No matter how hard I tried, I always failed him." Tears pooled in her eyes, and she dashed them away impatiently.

"Until he introduced me to Stanley." Revulsion and a lingering hint of the fear she'd undergone at Stanley's hands skittered across her skin, and she shivered. "Dad loved Stanley. He encouraged me to date him and to marry him. He didn't want to hear that I didn't love Stanley. This was a business merger. A way to blend two enormous financial entities into one all-powerful unit. I never should have agreed to marry a man who didn't love me, a man who I didn't even like. But I did. I married him, and for a while, my father was proud of me."

She swallowed hard, choking down a lump of emotion that threatened to block her words.

"I learned fast I'd never live up to Stanley's expectations, either. He had all the same complaints as my father. Too fat, too crude, too quiet, too friendly with the staff. It didn't matter what I did, it was always too…too something. God, I was so miserable. Then Stanley took to drinking more and more, and when he drank, he got angry."

She shuddered and huddled into herself but refused to stop her story. "Mean and violent. He hit me. Often." She looked at Clint, trying to judge his reaction.

He looked upset, almost irate, but there was a soft light in his eyes. He was upset but not with her. Natalie almost laughed when Clint growled low in his throat.

"I was going to leave him when I found out I was pregnant. Then I became a virtual prisoner in my own home. I was trapped. Stanley put guards on me whenever I left the house. He changed the alarm code so I couldn't leave undetected." Anger made her voice rise. "When he threatened to harm Mathew, all bets were off. I secreted away money and stole some of Eugenia's tranquilizers. Then when Stanley was drunk and celebrating crushing yet another small company under his heels, I drugged him, packed up, grabbed Mathew and bolted."

Her breath was ragged, the remembered fear of that night bearing down on her, threatening to overcome her. "Then I crashed my car, and you showed up."

Clint interrupted. "And I looked over the crest of that hill, and there you were, a filthy, tattered angel. Trying her best to save her son. God, you were beautiful, but so scared."

"I'm not finished."

"My turn." Clint took her hand in his and stroked her palm softly. "You were beautiful but so unsure, so scared. I think that's when I fell in love with you." He sighed and smiled. "But you rebuffed me at every turn. I could tell you liked me, but you had so much baggage, so many fears."

"I was married to a beast. I wanted you, I needed you, but part of me was still afraid."

"I knew that." His fingers traced hers. "It was a long time before you told me about your past, but God, I admired you. Working so hard to make a go of it, struggling to find your way and fend for yourself. And then you let a few things slip, and I realized I might know who your husband was. Jesus, it freaked me out. Knowing you'd grown to despise the life you lived with my half-brother. How could I tell you who I was? How could I risk you walking away and destroying my heart?"

"You should have told me." Her fear and anger subsided slowly with his words, but she was still uncertain.

"I should have. I'm not like them. I've never been like my family. But Genie? Genie was a wonder. She invited me into her home. She was gracious and caring, even though I was a bastard sired by her cheating husband. Genie is how I knew Mathew would be safe at home. So, I took him there, against your wishes, because I knew he needed familiar territory."

"Why didn't you bring him back to Haven?" Natalie accused. "He loves it here."

"Too far away." Clint rose from the bench and walked around the picnic table without releasing her hand. "I needed to be near you, in case you needed me." He sat beside her and held her hand between both of his.

He looked so sincere, so afraid she might reject him. He did love her, and he wasn't anything like the other men in her life. Her heart soared.

"Stop." She bit back a grin when Clint's tentative smile turned into a massive frown. She stood and stepped back from the table. Then she dropped to her knees beside him and grasped his hands.

"We both made some horrible mistakes and told some lies. I want this to end." She almost laughed at the panic that contorted his face. "Shh." She gripped his hands tightly. "I might be going to jail for a murder I didn't commit, but by God, I want you to know something first. I love you, Clinton James Dawson. I love you, and I want to marry you. Will you marry me and look after my son— our son—if they haul me off to jail? Will you wait for me?"

"Yes!" Clint shouted and leapt to his feet, dragging her from her knees, grabbing her in a hug and spinning her around until they toppled over onto the ground.

He lay there, atop her, planting tiny kisses all over her face, her cheeks cupped in his hands. "I love you, Natalie. I love you more than anything. I'll marry you, and I'll look after Mathew if the unthinkable happens."

He kissed her deeply, and his love poured into her, filling up the hollows in her heart. She kissed him back, showing him, without words how deeply he moved her, how much she loved him.

The sound of cheering and clapping surrounded them, and they bolted to their feet.

"About damned time." Lisa moved in to hug them.

"Damned right," Grace and Sterling chimed in unison.

Natalie and Clint looked around. Half of Haven stood clustered around them, their faces wreathed in smiles.

"Apparently, a helicopter in Haven draws a crowd." Clint laughed and kissed Nat deeply, making the crowd roar with approval.

The muffled sound of her phone ringing distracted Natalie. She ignored it, and it stopped only to start again. She backed away from Clint and rummaged in her purse for her cell. It vibrated in her hand and rang again. She looked at the display which read Vancouver police. She became lightheaded, and she stopped breathing. She wavered unsteadily and clutched Clint for support.

Was this it? Was this the end to their brief happiness?

"Answer it." Clint read the display over her shoulder. "Whatever it is, we'll deal with it together."

She nodded mutely and answered the phone, choking out a hello.

"Is this Natalie Walker?"

"Yes."

"This is Detective Strong of the Vancouver police department. We met on your case."

"Yes?" *Shit. They don't want me back in Vancouver, do they?*

"I called to tell you we've arrested your late-husband's secretary for his murder." He explained the situation briefly and then said goodbye.

Natalie kept her face carefully neutral despite dancing inside. She turned and looked solemnly at Clint.

"What?" He grabbed her shoulders and gave her a small shake. "Tell me, Natalie."

"It was the police."

The crowd gasped.

"The officer said… said…" She took a deep breath.

"What?" Clint shouted.

"They found the woman who killed Stanley." She gave a whoop of excitement. "I'm free!"

"Who killed him?" Clint asked.

"They've arrested his latest mistress, Alisha." Natalie smiled in relief.

Clint pulled her into his arms and kissed her soundly. Before she realized what he was doing, he'd grabbed her by the arm, pulled her through the crowd, around the building and toward his trailer.

"What?" She tried to dig in her heels, but he pulled her along, despite her resistance.

"We're celebrating." He kissed her deeply and pulled her into his embrace before dragging her inside the trailer and laying her gently on the bed.

Slowly, he leaned over and kissed her. "I love you, Natalie Walker."

Her heart jumped and started pounded. She'd been waiting for this. Almost from the first time she'd seen him, she'd wanted to kiss him, to make love to him. His patient acceptance of her uncertainty and her married status had only made that yearning grow. Now, she could give in to it, she could accept the love he offered.

"Make love to me, Clint." She trailed her fingers across his lips and down to toy with the buttons on his shirt.

"Gladly," he whispered against her lips.

Slowly, gently, they explored each other, getting to know their likes and wants, and the little pleasures that fueled their passions until finally they soared together and drifted slowly back to earth.

In a small vestibule in the back of Haven's mixed denomination church, Natalie and her three bridesmaids chatted excitedly as they finished her final preparations for the wedding. Excitement skittered down Natalie's spine.

She hugged her friends close. "Thank you so much for being here for me."

"Wouldn't miss it for the world." Lisa laughed. "I've waited a long time for someone to catch Clint's eye."

"How could I miss seeing my employee and friend get married?" Grace hugged Natalie again.

Three solid thumps sounded at the door. The group looked back and forth at each other. Belinda went over and opened it a crack.

"I need to see Natalie," Mac's voice boomed out.

"Nope."

"I'm an RCMP officer, and I need to see her."

"I don't care who you are," Belinda said. "Nobody sees the bride before the wedding."

Natalie smiled at her friend's staunch defense.

"I don't care about silly traditions. I'm an officer of the law, and I need to talk to Natalie."

"Let him in," Natalie said to Belinda. "If he says he needs to see me, it must be important."

Belinda took a small step back and shook her finger in Mac's face. "Don't you fuck up this wedding, or I'll have your balls for breakfast."

Mac burst into laughter. "Honey, you only weigh a quarter of nothing. There's no way you could take me."

Natalie glanced back and forth between her friends. Mac looked as if he'd swallowed something distasteful, and anger contorted Belinda's face. Despite that, Natalie could almost see the sparks exploding between them. This could prove to be interesting. Later.

"All right, guys. Let's not delay this wedding. I've waited too long for this." When neither friend moved, she gently pushed Belinda past Mac so he could enter. When he managed to step inside, she ushered Lisa and Grace out the door and closed it behind them, shutting her maid of honor and bridesmaids out of the conversation.

"What do you want, Mac?" Natalie prayed he didn't have bad news.

He stammered for a moment, and she wanted to shake the words out of him.

"I came to apologize." He looked at the floor and blushed.

"For what?"

"For arresting you. I didn't think you'd done it, but it's my job, and I can't let friendship interfere with my job."

Natalie patted his shoulder and smiled. "It's okay, Mac. You wouldn't be part of this ceremony if I hadn't already forgiven you. Go on now." She pushed him toward the door. "Check on Clint."

"Clint's a wreck." Mac laughed. "He's worried you'll change your mind, but I know better. You love him to bits. Thanks for forgiving me." He walked out of the room.

"Get away, you oaf." Belinda shoved her way past Mac and back into the room with Lisa and Grace hot on her heels.

"That man is infuriating," Belinda huffed. "Interrupting your preparations for…for that!"

Natalie laughed. "He's a strange one. Mac worries about a lot of things, but he's a good man."

"He's an oversized brute."

"Help me with my veil." Natalie changed the subject.

Lisa smoothed the heavily beaded silk of Natalie's dress into place while Grace put the last few pearl-tipped pins into Nat's hair. Gently, Belinda attached the veil and draped it over Natalie's face.

"Perfect," the women said together, their voices a breathless sigh.

Natalie hugged them. "Thanks for being here. And remind me later that I have an idea to run by you guys. I want to build a place for abused women. I need your help."

"You're thinking about other women? Today?" Belinda stared at her.

"I am. Too many women are going through what I went through." Natalie smiled. "It's crazy that despite everything, Stanley had me in his will and I'm a controlling partner in Walker Enterprises. I won't run the company, and I'm going to promote the VP to president, but there will be changes. Walker Enterprises is going to be less about profit and more about helping people. There's a crap load of stuff to figure out, but we're working on it. I'm going to use his money to help other people."

"That would piss Stanley off." Lisa laughed.

"I think of it as retribution for all the trouble and suffering he caused."

A voice outside called through the door, asking if they were ready. Natalie nodded.

"Let's get this show on the road." Belinda clapped her hands together.

The Wedding March started, and Mathew, the ring bearer,

headed up the aisle followed by Amy, the flower girl. Next came her bridesmaids, Lisa, Grace and Belinda.

Closing her eyes to savor the moment and the precious gift of this wedding and Clint's love, Natalie hesitated at the back of Haven's small church sanctuary.

She opened her eyes and lifted her head. Clint was staring at her from beside the altar.

He looked awestruck and perfect.

So handsome with his neatly trimmed hair, clean-shaven face and perfectly pressed suit. But it was the expression on his face that made her feet move. He seemed…smitten. As if he couldn't wait to hold her. His love for her shone like a beacon, drawing her forward, and she slowly moved up the aisle, past the pews decorated in bright daisies, white and green ribbon and baby's breath. Past their friends and most of Haven.

She moved slowly, carefully, storing every memory.

Clint bolted forward and scooped her into his arms. She giggled in surprise.

"You're moving too damned slow." He laughed and set her back on her feet in front of the minister. He kissed her soundly through her veil.

"Mr. Clint said a bad word," Mathew exclaimed in shock, and the entire congregation chuckled.

"Tsk, tsk, Clint." The minister gave him a mock glare. "No kissing until you've finished your vows."

"To heck with that." Clint kissed Natalie again.

"Patience." Natalie grabbed his hand.

His sigh trembled through her.

"I love you. I'm not going anywhere."

It took only minutes to recite their vows and for Clint to slowly raise her veil and welcome her into his world with a kiss.

His lips brushed across hers slowly, gently, then he clutched her to his chest and devoured her mouth until the minister cleared his throat.

Natalie laughed against his lips, and Clint scooped her into his arms and strode down the aisle and out of the church. There, outside, in private, he kissed her again.

"I love you, Mrs. Dawson." He sighed happily and tightened his embrace.

Joy flooded through her. Here she was, at last, with the man of her dreams; the man who'd make her happy, love her, cherish her and surprise her with good things. Forever.

Did you enjoy this book?
If you did, please consider leaving a review on the platform of your choice.
Reviews are an author's life blood.

ABOUT KATIE O'CONNOR

Katie O'Connor lives in Calgary, Alberta, Canada. She married her high school sweetheart and is living her happily ever after. She is the mother of two grown daughters and is extremely proud of her five grandchildren. She has two wonderful sons-in-law and a large support network of friends, family and fellow authors.

Katie's career path has been long and twisted, with most of her life devoted to her family. She's been a waitress, chambermaid, cashier, store manager, as well as a lab and x-ray technician. She is an avid quilter and crafter.

She's dabbled in writing since high school because something drives her to create stories. She swears that it's impossible for her NOT to write. Unsatisfied with one genre, Katie writes contemporary romance, erotic romance and erotica. Recently, she's crafted her first cozy mystery with the intention of publishing a cozy mystery series.

She believes in all things magical; including dragons, fairies, UFOs, ghosts, and house pixies. But most of all she believes in love, romance and hope.

Katie likes to make it up as she goes along and dreams of publishing a mixed genre novel. It is going to be an erotic, shape shifter, vampire, steampunk, sci-fi, murder mystery, adventure, romantic, western, historical, thriller. It will be her biography.

CONTACT KATIE O'CONNOR

Katie loves to hear from her readers.
Feel free to contact her anytime.

Website: https://katieohwrites.com
Email: katie@katieohwrites.com
Facebook: http://www.facebook.com/katieohwrites

Reviews are an author's life blood.
To thank readers generous enough to leave a review, I hold a
monthly draw for a free e-book. To enter, simply email me the link
to your review. (katie@katieohwrites.com)
Each month's winner will receive the e-book of their choice from
Katie's publications.

Thank you in advance, Katie.